A living dead man, tortured beyond recognition. A suitcase crammed with a million dollars in fresh, green currency. An eerie island. A sadistic millionaire. An exotic girl who knew all the answers, but whose lips didn't look as if they had been kissed as often as her manner indicated.

THAT'S WHAT SAM CAMERON SAILED INTO. THAT, AND MURDER—MURDER AND MORE MURDER.

MILLION DOLLAR MURDER

Edward S. Aarons

A FAWCETT GOLD MEDAL BOOK
Fawcett Publications, Inc., Greenwich, Conn.
Member of American Book Publishers Council, Inc.

Chapter One

NOW THAT HE WAS APPROACHING JOURNEY'S end, he gave himself up to thoughts and dreams of her. The sloop sailed herself, spirited and responsive, as sensitive to the touch of his hand as Nora herself had once been. Thinking of her, remembering the golden image of her and the crazy haze of days and nights that followed their first meeting, he faced himself, Sam Cameron, and decided he was a fool. Maybe not quite such a fool as he insisted. Nora was an experience worth any amount of despair and agony afterward. Every man had his Nora, Sam thought. If he never met her, he never fully lived. He had met her, known her, possessed her—or had all the possession belonged to her?—and he had lost her. Now he would see her again.

During the long, lazy days of cruising alone up from Long Island Sound, through the Sandwich Canal and across Massachusetts Bay, he knew his course had been inevitable. Gloucester had claimed him for only a day, and then the deep impatience in his vitals urged him northward again toward Maquid Point and Haddamsport. He was through pretending that the trip was merely a vacation from the boatyard. Ostensibly, of course, he was coming north on business. The ownership of the boatyard had to be settled, once and for all. Lyman, as a partner, was an anchor around his neck. He had to make Lyman, his brother, see reason. The fact that Nora had married Lyman Cameron, and not himself, was beside the point. He knew where Nora was, and he was going there, come hell or high water. He had to see her again.

The sloop sailed on, and he loafed at the tiller, dreaming, one part of him aware of wind and sky and sea, but the most of him absorbed in Nora, in memories and anticipation. He didn't see the dory until it was fairly close ahead.

The dory rocked and dipped and lifted and fell in the gray seas that marched out of the southeast. The sky reflected the sullen temper of the water. The light from the setting sun was flimsy, of an uneasy yellowish texture that darkened beyond the nearby headland. It was cold on the water. The wind blew in strong puffs that drove the sloop down hard on the drifting dory.

Sam touched the mainsail with an uneasy eye and watched the little derelict. The Holiday trembled, restless in this weather under her weight of sail, and her rudder transmitted the contrary forces of tide and wind to Sam's sensitive fingers. The dory seemed empty. Still, if it were from a wrecked dragger or a lobsterman adrift in these treacherous Maine waters, a survivor might huddle for shelter below the gunwales. He shifted course to scud before the wind and waited for the sloop to cover the distance.

Slightly to port, the low, burned-over back of Maquid Point was like the humped outline of a whale, and beyond was a glimpse of islands scattered like a handful of pebbles off the mainland. On the hazy shore to westward was the tiny fishing village and resort of Haddamsport, nestled among a wilderness of pine woods, sand dunes, and rock.

Light winked and shattered from the brow of Maquid Point. He looked there, but he was still too distant for any details to have definition. He wished now he had taken a deckhand on the cruise. He risked jibing by bringing the wind directly astern, slacked off on the jib sheet, and let the Holiday coast down the swells toward the drifting dory.

It still looked empty. Probably, he thought, it had just

worked free from a wharf or beach nearby. It wasn't worth the maneuver necessary to bring it alongside. He could see the painter trailing in the water, and the uneasy roll and splash of the lonely little boat made the thole-pins creak. Overhead, a gull swooped and screamed and flapped away again.

Sam frowned.

Something that looked like a shapeless bundle of blue clothing lay in the bottom of the dory, rolling with the roll of the boat. He just glimpsed it and then the dory slid down and away, the gray-green water heaving up between them. When he looked back, the dory seemed as lifeless and empty as before.

Soft dance music from his portable radio yielded to an announcer's spurious enthusiasm for soap, and Sam reached over and snapped it off. The wash and surge of the sea made the silence deeper and lonelier.

The jib slapped a sudden warning as the wind eased to the port quarter. Sam moved the tiller, heading up. Then, on sudden impulse, he swung the sloop all the way over and spilled wind from the mainsail. The Holiday shook herself, took on a new vibration as she plunged and tossed spray, beating off close-hauled toward the dory. The maneuver had put a wide reach of water between the two boats. For a moment he lost the dory, and then its narrow stern heaved up over a ridge of green and he bore down on it.

When he was abeam he turned full into the wind; the sails slapped and streamed as the sloop hung in stays for a shuddering instant, then drifted astern. He felt a warm pride in the boat's performance and delicacy. Hanging to the wind, the Holiday slid alongside the dory, almost close enough to touch it; and when the small boat slid down a sea directly along the quarter, Sam reached for the trailing painter. The water was icy. He shivered and made the line fast to the stern mooring cleat and hauled the dory closer.

A whining sound came from the bundle of blue clothing cramped in the dory's bottom. A thin, broken hand with twisted fingers lifted and groped upward in blind fashion. The hand closed on air and fell to the thwart again.

The sloop chose that moment to fall off the wind and sail again. For an anxious minute he was busy with tiller and sheets, bringing her back on course for the whaleback shape of Maquid Point. The light winked again on the distant hilltop. Perhaps it was only the reflection of a window—or it might be the glint of a glass that watched him. He thought of Nora again in that moment. She was there, somewhere on that headland, and he couldn't resist the thought of her and the swift excitement of seeing her again. Up to this point, where he had identified the thing in the dory as a human being, he still had a choice. He could have turned back. Now, because of the dory, he no longer had a choice. He was going to land on Maquid and see Nora again—Nora and his brother, Lyman.

It was tricky business, transferring the man from the dory to the Holiday's cockpit. He made the tiller fast and let the sloop run on her course, bearing for the far shore of the headland. The man in the dory was incredibly light and thin in Sam's arms. What spark of life remained seemed to have flickered out in that one gesture he'd made with his hand. Sam eased him down on the seat and stood looking at him. A cold, crawling shudder worked in his stomach.

This was no native fisherman suffering exposure or thirst. Sam was a boat builder, not a doctor, but he could see that something more was wrong with the man.

One by one, his mind tabulated the shocking physical damages. Revulsion squirmed inside him. The hand, first. Freshly broken, each finger swollen an ugly purple, jagged splinters of white bone sticking through the flesh. The bare feet, bloody and torn, scarred and purpled by small vicious burns. The left arm had been broken not quite so recently, and poorly set. The ribs were discolored by ugly welts and bruises. Two fingernails had been torn from the right hand. And worse had been done to the man. Yet he lived. The whining started again, coming from the battered, swollen mouth, a sound pitched in two keys, rising and falling in a nightmare world of torment behind the man's wide, staring eyes that saw nothing of the sky and sea around him.

An old man, but certainly not a fisherman. The palms were smooth, the face white and untouched by the sun. His thin, wispy hair was plastered to his bony scalp. The blue nylon slack suit, though torn and incredibly filthy, was expensive. The man hadn't been out of his clothes for days, perhaps weeks.

The bulging blue eyes rolled and swung from side to side. Sam touched the old man gently.

"Can you hear me, old-timer?" he asked.

The whine became a shriek. The crippled body thrashed convulsively to escape the touch of his hand.

"I won't hurt you," Sam said.

The purple mouth opened and sucked air. "Hurt me?"

"You'll be all right now," Sam said.

For a moment the rolling eyes settled on Sam's lean face. A pure, clear hatred burned into Sam's gaze.

"Help—me," the old man said.

"Just a moment."

Sam ducked forward into the small cabin, littered with blueprints and draftsman's sketches. Rummaging in the medicine locker, his hands shook, and he shoved aside the first-aid kit and found a square, dark bottle of brandy. He wondered if he was going to be sick. He had seen horror in the war, but this was worse, this tortured old man driven mad by fear. He returned on deck, and what he saw wasn't possible. The old man had moved. He had rolled off the bench near the tiller and somehow crawled to the lee rail, his bloody head turned to watch the dark shape of Maquid Point move closer. A strong, steady stream of curses came from his stiff lips. At the sound of Sam's step he twisted back, the light in his rolling eyes wild, then growing dull.

"Lie down," Sam said. "You're safe now."

The old man turned and tried to fling himself over the side into the trailing dory. Sam grabbed at him and hauled the weak, shaking body back aboard. For just an instant the man's crippled hands beat at him, as feebly as the beat of a butterfly's wings. The whining noise came from his mouth again. Sam eased him down.

"Who did this to you? What happened to you?"

The whining went on and on. There were smears of blood on the deck now, and Sam straightened and picked up the brandy bottle. It couldn't help the old man. Nothing could help him.

The light was fading when he nosed the Holiday into a small cove that opened in the rocky shore. He proceeded under jib alone, his senses sharpened to detect any sudden change in wind and tide. Far, far astern, a light winked on the darkening sea. The dory swung sharply in an eddy of tide and Sam eased the tiller over, wondering about the depth of water in the cove.

Then he saw that he need not have worried. As the cove opened before him, he saw the tall spars of a forty-foot schooner at her moorings ahead. Tied to a stone dock nearby was an open lobster boat, two dinghies, and a red motor launch. Plenty of water for the Holiday. The dock led to a graveled path that swung out of the scented pine woods and circled a boathouse and a small, red-painted sail loft. A string of lobster buoys made a bright beading against the gathering shadows.

No one was in sight. There was a faint, pungent odor in the air that made him wrinkle his nose. It was a scent he was to identify afterward with horror and nightmare. At the moment, he recognized it as charred wood, and he lifted his glance to the slope of the headland until he saw where a forest fire had burned itself out long ago, leaving a blackened army of burned stumps that slanted against the gray sky. On the brow of the hill was a forbidding mass of blackened concrete and buttressed walls, tumbled into ruin. He frowned, wondering at the wealthy eccentric who would choose this place for a summer home. The house where Nora and Lyman were staying as guests was hidden down the shore, beyond a rocky rise of land toward the mainland.

There was his business with Lyman, about dissolving their joint ownership of the Cameron Boatyard, but his thoughts turned persistently to Nora. Nora's deep and throaty voice, whispering to him in blue stillness, her eyes luminous with secret laughter and then dark and estranged with passion. The cool, soft, intimate touch of her hand, the bright halo of her feathery bronze hair, the incredible silky feel of her body. Nora walking beside him in the rain in Manhattan; Nora, in slacks and striped basque shirt, long magnificent and golden legs dangling from the float at the boatyard while he talked with too much enthusiasm about his latest design for racing sloops. Nora laughing, Nora dancing, and Nora in bed with him—and then marrying Lyman.

Too late to turn back now, Sam thought. It was like a sickness from which there was no escape. To be near her while Lyman mocked him was insufferable, and even when he first raised Haddamsport on the horizon, knowing she was there, he hadn't decided to see her, regardless of his business with Lyman and the necessity for settling accounts. But the old man in the dory had made the decision for him.

He looked at the tormented old man. He had fallen into some sort of coma, and Sam hoped there was a doctor somewhere on Maquid Point. If not, it would mean a trip to Haddamsport, lying to the south beyond the ridge of the headland—if the old man lived long enough.

With the Holiday made fast to the stone pier, he paused to cast a professional and critical eye on the black-hulled auxiliary schooner at her mooring cable. She looked expensive and over-rigged. He noted the polished brasswork, the mahogany planks, the beaminess of her hull. Her name was in gilt letters on the transom—Panther. Not new, but outfitted for leisurely cruising. You could go around the world comfortably enough in her, he decided.

The shadows were thick when he struck up the graveled path through the woods. A sense of urgency and worry over the old man lengthened his stride. He wondered where everyone on Maquid could be. There was no stir of life anywhere. The southeast wind moved the crowns of the pine trees, but failed to reach the rank undergrowth that crowded the path. The silence felt hot and oppressive.

The path led up through the woods and the scent of charred timber was stronger. He could see nothing ahead but the dark shrubbery, and after the first bend, the cove and the boats were cut off from sight behind him. He paused suddenly and listened. There was nothing to see or hear. He wondered at the uneasiness that filled him, and put it down to the prospect of seeing Nora soon, visualizing her surprise, anticipating her reaction.

The path dipped into a narrow ravine. The darkness was almost that of night, a dense smoky blackness through which the way bored like a tunnel. Yet he saw the shadow behind him, and heard the quick crunch of footsteps on the gravel. He had no time to turn, to verify the quick, shrieking alarm inside him. No time to do anything, really.

The shadow had an arm upraised, holding something thick and blunt, and then fire and pain descended upon him.

Chapter Two

HE DREAMED OF RUNNING ENDLESSLY, WITH horror breathing at his heels. For a time he found himself the old man in the dory, with sightless, marble-blue eyes, as sound came from him in intolerable length, forced by the pain. He felt a terror he had not known since his childhood nightmares, and an imagery haunted him, distorted and insane. And all the time the footsteps ran after him, implacably pursuing, as if death itself raced with him through a surrealist landscape.

Sometimes he knew he was dreaming and struggled to cast off the tortured body of the old man he inhabited. Other times, he knew that what was happening was real, that the fire-charred forest of naked, tilted trees existed, and he was running through it, uphill, toward the seared and blackened walls of an ancient structure that reared up out of a moonlit sea. He fell and picked himself up and fell again. He scrambled over huge, buttressed foundations and found himself in a nave of a ruined church, skeletal, roofless, open to wind and sky, violently lonely. The footsteps moved back and forth, seeking him in the black shadows. He stumbled on, along the lip of a bluff over-hanging an angry sea, and through the blind pain in his mind he asked himself why, and what he had done. And there was no answer.

In the end he was overtaken. Before him was a drop into darkness, and a shimmering black pool waited far below. He turned and faced his pursuer; but it was just a shadow against the velvet of the sky, moving toward him. He remembered his pain, the wild panic that insisted on flight. He couldn't fight back. If he tried, he would lose, and that would be the end of it, and he would never know why this had been done to him, or who had done it. Turning, he threw himself forward and down into the dark pool below.

He waited in darkness for all time. . . .

Slowly it became light. A glimmer at first, but he strug-gled up to it as if the darkness were made of some thick, viscous stuff reluctant to let him go. His head ached. He felt bruised and battered and utterly spent, a feeling so alien that his panic returned, and with it the insane fear that somehow he and the old man in the dory were one and the same.

Sam opened his eyes. He lay still, the monstrous terror quivering inside him. Sunlight made little ripples over his head, casting down bright spears of light. For a long time he lay suspended between nightmare and reality, studying the ribbed wooden ceiling overhead, the ripples of warm sunlight reflected off varnish, the brass lamp that hung steady in its gimbals. He was in a cabin, but he was not on a boat. It had been evening, and now there was day-light. He closed his eyes, remembering. Through the pulse of pain in his head he returned to the sea, the sloop and the old man, and then the deserted cove at twilight. The dream flickered through his mind again. But was it a dream? His head pounded. He sat up, shuddering. From a long way off, a voice said irritably:

"Lie still, won't you?"

He looked around. He saw no one. The room, or cabin, was empty and utterly strange. Nothing in the past could touch the present confusion inside him. It was daylight. Morning. The sunlight that flickered on the ceiling came through open windows, reflecting from water that lapped below and from beyond, from a glare of brilliant blue sea. But there was none of the movement of a boat, and he knew he was in a house of some sort, built over the beach, so that at flood tide there was water beneath; the slosh and pull of its bubbling filled the air.

One thing at a time, he thought. He was still alive. He pushed the memory of charred forest and ruined church and deadly pursuit out of his mind. Begin with the here and now, he told himself. Something had begun with the act of rescuing an old man with broken hands and a tortured body—something that had stolen the night from him and the everyday reality of the world. Something not good.

He sank back into the cool sheets of the bunk. The pain ebbed and flowed in his head. Deliberately he forced himself to relax while he studied the room. An ordinary room, with chintz curtains, wicker furniture, pine paneling partially covered with photographic prints of sailing vessels. The air of tidiness, of everything being trim and ship-shape, reassured him. Nothing bad could happen to him here. Whatever it was he had gone through, it was over for the moment.

He thought of the tortured old man, of his sloop, of Nora. He smoothed his palms down over his ribs, surprised to find himself nude under the cool sheets. Somewhere bacon popped and crackled in a skillet, and he smelled the warm pungency of strong coffee. Beyond the windows, a horde of gulls screamed and mewed. He sat up again. Someone had spoken to him.

"Hello!" he called.

A clattering came from the kitchen beyond the doorway. Quick footsteps tapped, and a girl stood there looking at him. His heart jumped, thinking it was Nora; and then he saw that she wasn't Nora at all. He had never seen this girl before.

He found himself smiling.

"I'll say it," he began. "Where am I?"

"My house. How do you feel?"

"Alive. That's about all."

"You're lucky," the girl said. Her eyes were sober. "A fool for luck. I almost killed you."

"You?"

"When I found you in my boat, the Emma G."

Confusion again. He had a crazy urge to get up and look at himself in the mirror to make sure he wasn't the old man. He looked at the girl instead. Her dark hair was rich and thick and gleaming softly where it curled about her tanned, bare shoulders. She wore a playsuit of some rough blue material with little black figured cockers romping over it. Her legs were long, firm and smooth and tanned a deep, golden hue. She was young, Sam thought. He appreciated the clean curved lines of breast and thigh, just ripening to maturity. She was untouched, but not innocent. Her eyes were too bold, too defiant, too sullen.

"All through?" she asked, annoyed.

"I was just looking."

"It's not for you," she said.

He laughed. There was a sulky droop to her mouth, and her dark blue eyes held a sullen look that was almost hostile.

"All right. What happened to me?" he asked.

She shrugged. "You were drunk. You hit yourself on the head. You fell into the water."

"No," Sam said.

"Then you tell me."

"But where is Nora? And Lyman?"

She said: "I don't know them. Look, Mr. Cameron, you get your clothes on and have breakfast and we'll figure it out. We'll get you back where you belong. I'm a good Samaritan, all right, but only up to a point. And the point is that you seem to be capable of taking care of yourself from here on out. I don't want you cluttering up my house.

I don't like the way you look at me, either. Last night you were drunk and you pulled yourself out of the water into my boat and you scared hell out of me when you came for me."

"What did I do?" Sam asked.

"You thought I was somebody named Nora." Her mouth was sullen. "You tried to make love to me. Then you tried to kill me."

He was shocked. "No."

"You passed out before I had to take steps to stop you. Get your clothes on and I'll take you back to your friends. And good riddance."

Her stubborn contempt and hostility made him want to slap her. He told himself to go slow. Lack of patience would get him nowhere. He was faced with a jigsaw puzzle in this thing that had happened last night, and he would have to wait to get all the pieces in his hands before the picture clarified. He sat still, holding the bedsheet around him; the girl returned to the kitchen.

"Hurry it up," she said.

He tried to remember her b——
There was nothing between his plunge into the dark water and right now. He had not seen her before. He tried to reconstruct a logical pattern of events to fill the gap. A state of shock would do it, letting him act and talk as if fully conscious, climbing into her boat and thinking she was Nora. Nora was always in his mind.

He touched the back of his head and winced. Someone had slugged him. He hadn't been drunk. Maybe this girl thought he'd been drunk; and she didn't approve. But that was no explanation. Getting up, he conquered a moment of dizziness and groped into a tiny bathroom. It was as trim and spotless as the other room, with a big mirrored medicine cabinet. Four toothbrushes hung in a rack beside the soap dish, and there was a razor and shaving kit. She didn't live here alone. He wondered if she were married. She wore no ring. He frowned, realizing he didn't even know where "here" was.

He found his wrist-watch and wallet on a shelf under the cabinet. His money and papers were intact. He took two aspirins and examined the bruises on his body with growing anger. An idea stirred in the back of his mind and he stood very still in the hot morning calm, staring at himself. Once, not too long ago, he had wanted to kill Nora. Maybe he still wanted to. Maybe—

He looked at himself in the mirror again. He looked normal enough. He had never been especially conscious of his appearance, but now he studied himself with care, as if the answer to the idea could be found on his features. It was an ordinary face. He had thick reddish hair and weather-darkened skin and long crinkles around his gray eyes from staring at distant horizons too much. He looked about twenty-eight, and was thirty-one. He was tall, but not over six feet; in good condition from long hours of outdoor work, of sailing and building the boats he designed. Nothing but boats had ever interested him, ever since he could remember. Along the Sound, his reputation as a successful, if somewhat unorthodox, designer of racing sloops was sound. As a marine engineer, Sam Cameron had led an ordinary life—except for Nora, of course—and he could think of nothing to explain what had happened last night.

But the idea grew in the back of his mind, the idea that someone had seriously tried to kill him.

Someone had been watching when he was still far out to sea, when he picked up the derelict dory. He remembered the wink of light reflecting from glass on Maquid Point. Someone had watched him moor the Holiday in the cove and leave the old man. And had followed him and tried to kill him.

Sam lowered his towel and leaned on the wash basin. His hands shook. Perhaps the same person had done those things to the old man in the dory. And where was the old fellow now?

A sense of urgency quickened inside him, and he cast about impatiently for his clothes. He couldn't find his own. But there was a pair of dungarees and sneakers and a white skivvy that would do. The dungarees were too wide in the waist and the sneakers too small, but he squirmed into them and went to seek the girl.

She wasn't in sight, but she had set up a card table and used a checkered tablecloth and his breakfast stood on it, a plate of Canadian bacon and eggs and a gray enameled coffee pot supported by an iron trivet. He went into the kitchen, a long narrow room with a screened window overlooking the water. She stood by the window, looking down at something he could not see, but which she watched with a look of virulent hatred that seemed shocking on her young, healthy face. His approach in sneakered feet was soundless, yet she whirled, her dark blue eyes wide and startled.

"Don't sneak up on me like that!" she snapped.

"Why so jumpy? I'm the one who's all the sixes and sevens. What's down there?"

"Where?"

"On the water."

He moved to her side and looked. There was nothing on the water. But he heard the sound of a motor, and there was a faint wash that might have been the wake of a passing boat. The boat was out of sight, hidden behind a rickety wooden wharf and spit of sandy shore. He saw for the first time that this house was built on the southern beach of Maquid Point, facing the long arc of hazy shore that stretched toward Haddamsport. He had anchored on the opposite side of the whaleback headland last night. He shook his head and turned back to the girl.

"How did you know my name?"

"I looked through your clothes and your wallet. Why not? Your pants are on the line, drying, incidentally. I'm Ferne."

"Ferne what?"

"Just Ferne. It's good enough for you."

"Look," he said. "Did you put me to bed last night?"

She flushed faintly. "I had help."

"That's what I need. Help. You know I wasn't drunk last night. Have some coffee with me and take the chip off your shoulder, Ferne. Tell me about last night. Please," he urged.

She hesitated, still hostile. Her attitude seemed to be at odds with her hospitality, Sam decided. Anyway, he owed her his life. He wondered what made her so jumpy and what she had seen through the window that had filled her with such naked hatred. Then the girl shrugged and said: "Your bacon is getting cold. Sit down and eat. I'll have coffee with you, if you insist."

He was surprised to find himself hungry. The aspirin had dulled the headache, and somehow he liked this clean bright room and the colored pottery on the table and the way Ferne's hair curled about her smooth shoulders. A photograph in a silver frame stood on a pine chest of drawers against the wall—a thin young man with a sober look, in a Navy uniform. Sam nodded at it.

"Your brother?"

"No."

"You're not married, are you?"

"No."

He got up and looked at the inscription on the photo. *To Ferne—forever yours—Alex*. He spoke over his shoulder.

"Did Alex ever come back?"

Her voice flattened. "No. Alex was the kind who wouldn't."

He returned to the table in a silence and poured coffee from the gray pot first into his cup, to dispose of the grounds, and then filled hers. The coffee was strong. He began to eat, disregarding the girl's steady, puzzled gaze. Suddenly she said: "You have a fine boat, you know."

"The Holiday? Have you seen her?"

"She's yours?"

Sam nodded. "I built her. This is her first cruise. Tell me—you saw me come in last night, didn't you?"

She hesitated. "No, I didn't."

"Someone watched me with glasses, from Maquid."

"It wasn't I."

She was lying. He felt it. "I've never been to Maquid before. My brother, Lyman Cameron, and his wife, Nora, are house guests of a man named Casper Varden, who owns most of this place, as I understand it. I've never met him. I didn't see anybody last night when I landed, but I was jumped in the dark and almost killed. I'd like to know who did it, and why."

Ferne's eyes slid away from him, down to the table and then sidewise toward the door. He went on:

"Next thing I knew, I woke up here. I don't know how I escaped the lad who lumped me; I have some memories that seem like a nightmare—a burned-over forest and a roofless church, and then I was running and dived into the water. That's about it. I wasn't drunk, Ferne, but I guess I was badly shocked. Whatever happened, I must thank you, because it looks like you saved me."

He paused. She wasn't listening to him. Her slim body had stiffened, and her head was cocked to one side, as if listening to something else. Sam heard it, too—the measured tread of boots coming up an outside wooden stairway. He was surprised at Ferne's pallor. He had seen her sullen, passionate face filled with hatred when she looked out the window. Now he saw that she was deeply and terribly afraid. The footsteps outside paused. The girl gave herself a little shake and tossed her long dark hair back over her shoulders. Her smile was a little twisted.

"I don't know anything about it," she said. Her voice was too loud. "You were in my boat when I came back to it, and you acted like a crazy man. I thought you were drunk, and I still think so. It was the least I could do, to put you to bed and let you sleep it off. That's all there was to it, for my part."

Sam said: "But there is more."

Something stirred in her eyes, but he couldn't tell if it was a plea or some inner anguish. It was quiet outside, except for the lap of water under the house and the mewing of the gulls.

"About three miles offshore," Sam said, "I picked up a drifting dory. An old man was in it. Somebody had worked him over thoroughly. He had been beaten and tortured until he was out of his mind. I brought him to the cove on the north shore of Maquid and I was going for help when I was waylaid. You were in that cove a little later, Ferne. I'm sure of it. Was anybody down there to look at my boat and take care of the old fellow?"

voice came back to him from under the muffling red canvas.

"Gasoline is a problem up here. Nate is always using my boat to go visiting, and he never puts a drop in the tank. Now I'll have to go all the way to Haddamsport for more."

Sam felt a perverse urge to stimulate her anger.

"That was a touching scene," he said. "Why does your father keep that brute working around here?"

"My father is Casper Varden." Ferne didn't look at him when she spoke. "He lives across the point. I guess your friends are staying with him. He's not my father, really— he's just a man who married my mother. She's been dead for two years. It was a bad mistake. Cas and I don't have much to do with each other. We don't get along."

"Who owns this place here?"

"I do. I keep it up. Cas and Nate would like to get the whole peninsula from me, but they'll have to kill me, first."

Sam said: "That's touching, too."

The engine roared into life and the girl came back to the wheel. Her face was white, and she didn't look or speak to him again. Sam cast off the stern and bow lines and sat on one of the lobster traps. Ferne kept her back to him, intent on maneuvering the boat in a long wide sweep around the headland to the north shore. In the mid-morning light, the air was almost sharp enough for him to distinguish the distant cluster of houses that made up Haddamsport. He looked back and saw the slim figure of Eli Broom on the porch of the house that overhung the water. Broom was watching them, and when Sam turned his head, the man waved. He made no reply.

It was only a ten-minute run around the point to the other anchorage, accomplished in silence except for the laboring of the Emma G.'s ancient engine. The southeast wind had veered easterly, but the open sea beyond the headland had a treacherous chop caused by conflicting tide and wind. Sam was satisfied with the girl's sulky silence. The thought of seeing Nora soon filled him with the familiar excitement, so that he forgot Ferne and the puzzle of last night. The thought of his brother Lyman was something else again.

What do you do, he wondered, when you are in love with your brother's wife?

Memory came back to him, cutting new wounds over the old, criss-crossing the fabric of this quiet moment. It was almost a year ago, but he could remember the dress she wore, the way she sat at the bar in the nightclub, her face and figure a challenge and a lure, her eyes amused as Sam and Lyman quarreled. Sam was always quarreling with his older brother. As usual, it was about money and the boatyard. The money was needed for the business, for a chance to develop Sam's designing ideas. Lyman was no business man. Lyman had none of the usual responsibility of an older brother. He was handsome, he was smart, he was smooth and spoiled. This quarrel was a particularly nasty one, because Lyman chose to be that way, and finally the girl, Nora Jordan, slid smoothly from her seat and laughed at them and said:

"Why don't you two choose your weapons?"

"I'll take martinis," Lyman said instantly. "No, make it champagne. One doesn't meet Nora Jordan every day."

Sam had never heard of her, but at the moment he wished he had. Something queer gripped his stomach, just looking at her. Normally, it would be Lyman, with his smooth good looks and polish, who would occupy the girl's attention; and the way it usually worked, Sam would soon find himself alone. It didn't work out that way with Nora. Perhaps, perversely, it was because Sam didn't wear evening clothes as if he were born into them, and didn't know the latest yacht club gossip and wouldn't have repeated it if he did. Maybe she felt sorry for him. It was Lyman, circulating genially through the clubs and hangouts of the wealthy yachtsmen, who brought in the orders for new racing designs. Lyman was the smooth one, with the air and ability to move easily in Nora Jordan's circle. Lyman visited their houses and drank and golfed with them, and then told them why they hadn't won the last cup race, and suggested that Sam, his kid brother, was a kind of minor genius when it came to designing racing sloops. Lyman belonged with Nora Jordan. Yet she turned to Sam that night in the yacht club, and Lyman retreated after a few moments, baffled and angry.

"Take me somewhere, Sam," she said.

"Any place in particular?"

"Some place that's just you-and-me, Sam."

He remembered her apartment on Central Park South that night, the extravagance of it that was as bold as herself—the zebra-striped couch, the marble fireplace, the luxury of the Sarouk rug. The drive into Manhattan, in her custom-built convertible, was cool, taking the North Shore roads down and then across the Triboro Bridge. Nora's bronze hair was a pale flame in the night. Later, when they were alone, when they had achieved the you-and-me status, when they sat on a small terrace opening from that rich room and watched the stars wheel over Central Park, she told him about herself. She gave him fair warning, Sam remembered. She was honest with him, for some obscure reason that he never afterward figured out, though later he felt sure there was never a truthful word in her.

"You like me, don't you, Sam?" she asked.

"Sure," he smiled. "You leave me no choice." He was aware of her, of every soft and enticing inch of her. "I like you."

"But you wouldn't like me if you knew about me. Say, for instance, if I were just a grocer's daughter from an upstate village, with no money, no glamor, nothing but a desire to get away from a hateful and poverty-stricken environment."

"But that's not you," Sam said.

"That's what I was."

"It wouldn't make any difference."

"Darling," Nora said, "it would. Money may be the root of all evil, but it's also the basis for everything about me. I'm not a very good girl, Sam." Her eyes regarding him were oddly luminous in the starlight. "They say you are a genius with boats, darling. Will you make a lot of money, for both of us, Sam?"

"Does it mean that much to you?"

Her breath quickened on his cheek. "Everything, Sam. Everything."

"Nora." He was trembling. "Nora?"

She said: "You'll stay with me tonight, Sam."

It was settled as simply as that. There was a forwardness about her, and a bold simplicity about her attack, that was new to him. He had had his share of girls before. He had helled around in Europe and England during the war. He knew the Continental attitude toward love and sex, and Nora had it, either by instinct or education, and it didn't matter which. Her body met his with a passion that was like war, with an inventiveness and ingenuity that led him on and on, into dark whirlpools of passion, into blinding light and gasping hot depths where he lost himself and his identity, helpless and happy, ecstatic in his helplessness.

Fair warning. He should have been enough of a sailor to avoid flying into the teeth of a hurricane. But nothing like this had ever happened to him before. There had never before been a Nora Jordan in his life, and the emotional storms she brewed were hypnotic in quality. He tried to imagine her life in a small town such as she had described, her father rigorous and inhumanly stern; Nora in cotton dresses, watching the summer visitors, building up an overpowering drive to escape in any way possible. He thrust the images from his mind and pretended to forget them; he forbade her to raise ghosts again.

And then he heard about Amos Butterick.

He learned about it by a word here and there. Nothing outright, but enough to worry him increasingly. No one actually knew who Butterick was, except that he was exceptionally wealthy, a man of power, middle-aged. Butterick, someone said, was Nora's patron, financing her voice culture, paying her rent and bills. The knowledge came to Sam with sly, knowing grins, and partly veiled warnings that he was taking something that did not belong to him. He didn't ever meet the almost-mythical Amos Butterick, and Nora never mentioned him until Sam could endure his suspicions no longer and asked her bluntly about it.

She slapped his face and walked away from him that night.

Then, for five days, it was over. The laughter, the music, the passion was ended. The long walks in Manhattan, the lazy summer days at sea, loafing along under sail across the Sound—it was ended. The tempest bred maggots of jealousy in him, and he sulked in the boatyard. He lived there in a little two-room apartment adjoining his drafting rooms; he lived there and ate there and did no work at all.

On the fifth evening she came to see him. He wasn't expecting her. He lay in his bunk, hands clasped under his head, staring at the evening shadows in the room that smelled of sawdust and the sea, a hard, helpless ache inside him. And then she was there.

"Sam. Darling."

He looked at her, and her magic, black or white, was still potent.

"Sam, poor dear. You're being so silly."

"I don't think so," he said.

"You must not worry about Amos Butterick. It's silly to be jealous of a man who could be my father."

"But he isn't," Sam pointed out.

"He's been very kind to me. How old are you, Sam?"

"Thirty," he said.

Her mouth was a ripe lotus blossom, her face dim, her eyes alight as she leaned over him on the bunk.

"Old enough to know better, Sam," she whispered.

But he wasn't. It began all over again that night, the hunger for her that could only be appeased in one way. There was a peculiar anger and brutality in him. He kissed her and drew her down to him, and there was a little bubble of laughter caught between her shining teeth and a pleased bright light in her eyes. She slipped away from him, and with a gesture her dress vanished, and she stood before him without her clothes, her tawny body glistening, alive, shivering slightly.

"I need you, Sam. I want you."

He couldn't speak. She came back to him then, and it was as if they had been apart for years, not just five days.

"You'll stay with me," he whispered.

Her scented hair lay across his lips. "For tonight."

"For ever," he said.

"We'll see."

Two weeks later, Lyman entered the picture again. Sam remembered the scene very well—Lyman, handsome and arrogant in his cool white linens, one hip perched on Sam's drafting table in the boatyard office, his cool eyes somehow alien, his voice harsh.

"Sam," Lyman said, "you're making a fool of yourself."

"About what?" he asked.

"About Nora Jordan, of course."

"That's none of your business."

"I've made it mine."

Anger touched him. "Keep out of it. Nora is my girl."

"Don't kid yourself," Lyman smiled. "My dear boy, you are incredibly naïve. Someone has to lead you by the hand and show you the way. Nora is not your girl, Sam. Not yours."

Sam was dangerously quiet. "Then whose is she?"

"I know you've heard of Butterick. And he's heard about you, Sam. It gets around. People talk about it. All right. How do you think a girl like Nora, with no background, no family, no money, lives the way she does? Who bought her that apartment, that car, and her clothes? Sam, everybody knows what goes on. Nora is no good, she's a tramp, she and Butterick are . . ."

Sam hit him. It was the first time they'd fought since they were kids, and this was different from any other fight. Hatred exploded between them with Sam's hard, rope-calloused fist smashing into Lyman's smiling, handsome face. His blow drove Lyman backward, crashing through the trestle table and drawing board. When Lyman scrambled up, there was blood in his mouth, and he charged across the cluttered room, swinging. Sam hit him again, and once more, and didn't even feel Lyman's return blows. In a moment the office was a shambles. Lyman was bigger and heavier, but there was an edge of fat on his muscles that made him slower and weakened the murderous drive of his fists. Sam fought with a raging passion of despair, and the outcome was inevitable.

In the end, the explosion between them resolved into a deep, quiet pool of venom. Sam wrapped a handkerchief around his bloody knuckles and watched his brother crawl painfully upright, supporting himself on a broken chair, sucking air in great, shuddery gasps, his face a bloody mask of defeat.

"All right, Sam. Enough."

"Don't come here again," Sam flung at him. "We're through. I'll buy you out."

Lyman spoke through puffed, grinning lips. "Whenever you have the money, boy. Until then, I'll keep my share of the boatyard."

"I'm going to marry Nora," Sam said.

Lyman laughed. "No, you won't."

He went out, and Sam had the feeling that he had lost, somehow. That night was something like the night just past, Sam thought—unreal, vague, leaving him with the sensation of nightmare.

He had tried to telephone Nora. There was no answer. He locked up the wrecked office and drove the forty miles from Long Island to Manhattan, to her apartment house, and stood there ringing the bell in the warm twilight, not knowing what he would do if she wasn't there, not knowing what he would say if she were. He rang again, and finally the latch clicked and he went up in the elevator and a maid admitted him. The maid said Miss Jordan was not at home. He pushed past her and tore through Nora's rooms like a wild man. The maid stared. Probably she would have called for the police, if Nora's note hadn't stopped him.

Sam, darling, she wrote. *I warned you.*

He turned to the maid, pleading. "Where did she go? Tell me! What's she done?"

The maid didn't know. She was too terrified to speak. Sam flung himself out and began to look for Nora. He searched every place they had ever visited, from Greenwich Village to Harlem, and telephoned every mutual friend he knew. She was gone. He would have called

Amos Butterick, too, if he had known where to call, and
if he hadn't stopped to buy a morning newspaper. It was
after dawn by then, and all through the night he had
known something irrevocable had happened. The story
was in the newspaper, the tabloid, and he didn't want to
believe it.

Nora Jordan had eloped with Lyman Cameron, his
brother.

It didn't make sense. They scarcely knew each other.
She couldn't have been seeing Lyman all this time, without his knowledge. It wasn't true. But it was. It was true
then, and it was true now, a year later. . . .

FERNE DOLSON EASED THE WHEEL OF THE
Emma G. over to port and the lobster boat slid in almost
absolute silence through the still waters of the cove. Sam
breathed a quick sigh of relief when he saw the familiar
white hull of the Holiday untouched at the dock where he
had left her. The speedboat and schooner were also at
their moorings. But there was no sign of the dory he had
towed in.

As in the twilight of yesterday evening, no one was in
sight. The same narrow graveled path curved up into
the same pine woods, empty of life.

"Here you are," Ferne said.

"Yes."

He looked at her, but her face told him nothing except
that her temper had subsided. She looked almost worried
about him, and he wondered how pretty she would be if
she ever smiled. He doubted that Ferne smiled very often.
He watched her slim, supple figure as she leaned forward
and reversed the engine, then let it idle as the lobster boat
slid alongside the concrete pier. Sam leaped ashore. Immediately, Ferne gunned the motor and pulled out into the
cove.

"Thanks for the lift!" he called.

She kept the boat there, two fathoms of water between
them, and he could see the worry in her eyes as she
looked beyond him to the silent, wooded slope.

"Wait a minute," he called to her. "Why didn't you just

dump me in my boat here last night, instead of dragging me all the way around the point, if I was such a nuisance?"

Her voice came back clearly over the water.

"Because I knew you weren't just drunk, Mr. Cameron. Be careful, please!"

The roar of the old motor cut off his reply. He watched her until the lobster boat slid out of sight beyond the headland, and then he turned, frowning, and walked over to the Holiday.

An air of loneliness clung like a shroud over the little cove. Somewhere in the woods a robin called and a squirrel chattered. From farther in the distance came the mutter of surf on rocks.

Sam paused, examining his sloop with a slow, comprehensive glance that remembered the way he had left her last night. Everything seemed the same. Suddenly he shivered and whirled to face the wooded slope behind him. There was nothing to see. Nobody was there.

Stepping into the cockpit, he looked down at the square brown bottle of brandy on the floorboards. He hadn't used any of it on the old man, nor had he had a drink himself. The tax stamp should still be over the cork. Instead, there was no stamp and no cork. The bottle was empty.

Someone had washed down the dim, bloody footprints the old man had left on the deck, too.

After a moment he stepped down into the small cabin forward. He saw at once, in the dim light of the ports, that someone had been aboard, disarranging his orderly scheme of things for solitary sailing. Before he could move, a pair of soft, warm arms encircled his neck from behind him, and Nora's well-remembered voice whispered huskily in his ear.

"Sam, darling. I'm so glad you've come. I'm in terrible trouble."

Chapter Four

HER WORDS YIELDED TO SOFT, BREATHLESS laughter. Sam stood still, feeling the subtle excitement of her embrace, everything dissolving inside him. Nora Jordan Cameron. The year had been an eternity, and now it was only a moment, gone and forgotten.

"Sam, it's so good to see you again!"

She slipped around him, her knowing hands never leaving him, and now he could look at her and see that she was really Nora, the same Nora. She hadn't changed. Or if she had changed at all, she looked bolder, more beautiful, more striking than he had remembered. She wore a pair of dark blue slacks, tailored to her hips, and a sheer white shirt open deeply at the collar. He remembered more, and felt his throat close. Her auburn hair was like a distant brush fire, seen in the shadows of the tiny cabin. Her lips parted, uptilted to his, and she laughed breathlessly again, and her hands slid from his shoulders and she looked at him.

"Sam, I'm shaking so!"

"Is that all you have to say?"

Her eyes mocked him. He felt clumsy and awkward, unequal to her command of the situation, and he sat down with care on the steps leading down into the cabin, feeling his legs weak and unable to support him suddenly.

She said: "You came looking for me, at last. You did, Sam. Didn't you?"

"I came to see Lyman on business. I want to buy out his share of the boatyard. I can't keep it going, the way he siphons off the profits. I've got to settle with him or give it up."

"But you did want to see me, too, didn't you?"

"Yes," he said. "I couldn't help it."

"It took you a long time."

"Too long." He paused, searching his mind, forcing back the things he wanted to say, the questions he wanted to ask. He made his voice casual. "How did you know I was here, and that this was my boat, Nora?"

"Lyman noticed it last night. He said it was one of your designs. You can't imagine how I felt, darling. I slipped aboard and looked about at your things, and I knew."

"Didn't you wonder where I was, why the boat was deserted?"

"Of course. I was terribly worried. But this morning Nate came over and told us you were at Ferne's place, sleeping off a terrible drunk." Her voice softened. "Sam, you never used to drink much before."

"I wasn't drunk," he said briefly.

He waited, but she said nothing, sitting there and smiling, her hands clasped about her knees. He wanted to touch her, to hold her and possess her and pour out the agony of his year and forget the moment. He sat still. He looked at the wedding ring on her finger, and Nora's smile twisted.

"Poor Sam. What did I do to you?"

"You put me through hell," he said. "You poisoned me."

"And do you hate me for it?"

"No. I don't hate you, Nora."

The past flooded back, all the dreary months since he had lost her. He had hated her violently enough, at first. He hadn't seen her or Lyman since, but he heard a great deal. Enough to know that Lyman was edging closer and closer to the lie of illegality, with flashy friends, shady deals, and a sudden, unexplained affluence. Sam's own work declined. His designs were failures. He knew that despair was consuming him, but Nora's dark poison never lost effect. His hatred for her left him, but it was replaced by a sickness that destroyed him a little bit each day. He told himself she was wrong for him, that everything Lyman had said about her was true. He told himself many things, but because he didn't want to believe them, he denied them to himself.

"Don't look at me like that," Nora said.

"I was thinking. Wondering. Why did you marry Lyman?"

"But I told you. I warned you. If nothing else, I was honest with you about my past and my plans for the future. Nothing can change me, darling. I want good things, expensive things. Lyman got them for me. You couldn't."

"I might have, if you'd given me a chance."

"No, Sam, you wouldn't know how."

"Did you ever really love me?" he asked. "Did you love me at all, in the time we had together?"

She laughed softly. "Why do you think I'm here? Why have I been waiting alone, since dawn, for you to come back?"

He felt confused. There she was, without remorse, blandly sure of him, knowing him better than he knew himself. Oddly enough, he no longer felt injured. He had thought she was the same as he remembered her, but she was not. There were small differences. There were strange, unknown shadows behind her eyes, a tension in her face and figure that went beyond the feeling and straining between them. He spoke quietly.

"You said you were in trouble. What sort of trouble, Nora?"

"I don't know." She avoided his eyes. "Something is going on here. Something bad."

"But what is it?"

"I don't know. Lyman is mixed up in it and it's too much for him. He—Lyman isn't really strong, you know. He's not hard, inside and out, like you, Sam."

"What do you want me to do about it?"

She leaned forward. "Help us, Sam."

"I don't owe Lyman a thing."

"Then for me. You owe me nothing, too, I know. But I—I'd feel safer, knowing you were near me."

"Is it mixed up with that old man I picked up yesterday?"

"I don't know anything about it."

"But you heard about him?" Sam persisted.

"No."

Her reply came too quickly on the heels of his question. She didn't meet his eyes. She was frightened. Fear was not a familiar emotion in her, and she did not know how to conceal it. It was not an ordinary fear, either. Panic shuddered behind her smile. Sam leaned forward.

"Nora, what's really wrong? If you need help, you'll have to tell me about it."

"I can't."

"You can't—or you won't?"

She made a little gesture. "I just don't know enough. Please don't ask me about it, Sam. It's good just to know you're here, so providentially, and that I can count on you."

"But there *was* an old man, wasn't there?" he insisted.

She shook her head. Her smile was gone.

Sam said: "And last night, when I landed here, someone tried to kill me. He didn't succeed with the first blow, and somehow I got away from him, though I don't remember how. Ferne Dolson says she picked me up in her boat. You know who Ferne is, don't you?"

"Of course. She's Casper Varden's step-daughter."

"She saved my life," Sam said. "And she knows more than she's telling, too. Assuming that an old man really exists, who would he be? I mean, is there anybody from Haddamsport who is missing, or who fits that description?"

"No," Nora said. "I can't help you with it, Sam."

Sam leaned back, his face harsh and angular. "He needed help. He was desperately hurt. Maybe he crawled off this boat alone, but he couldn't have handled the dory, and it doesn't stand to reason that he could hide it, either. He was all but dead. I don't have any alternative but to go to the police with all this. Is there any reason why I shouldn't?"

"Yes," she said quietly. "A very good reason. You still love me, don't you, Sam?"

He looked at her. She waited. He said: "Yes, I still love you."

"Then that's reason enough. Because I ask you not to go to the police yet."

"Nora, you made a mistake."

"And it's too late to correct it now."

She smiled. She slid from the bunk and sat on the floor, at his knees, her face uptilted to his, her red hair flowing smoothly back around her shoulders.

"It's never too late, darling. Believe that. Some day, maybe soon . . ."

Twin emerald stones winked on the tiny lobes of her ears. A hunger grew inside him and could not be denied, as he remembered the shivering curves and shuddering hollows of her. He saw the warm light in her eyes, her triumph, and he hated her and leaned down and kissed her. Her mouth devoured him, her lips parted, sucking the vital life out of him. Her hands slid up under the short, loose sleeves of his skivvy shirt, smoothing his skin, her fingers tingling and exploratory, searching the muscles of his shoulders, sliding down his back. . . .

Lyman Cameron chose that moment to stumble aboard. Sam heard his footsteps and took Nora's hands from around him and twisted to look at the towering figure of his brother. Lyman was drunk. He stood with his yellow hair disheveled and his handsome features loose and uncertain, his eyes twisting from Sam to Nora. Nora slid back with a little sound and stood up and tried to step around him, out of the cabin. Lyman lurched sidewise and blocked her path. Nora's face was white.

"Let me go, Lyme."

He put his hand on her arm and held her back. Sam felt as if a spring were winding taut inside him. Lyman didn't look at him. His face was malevolent as he looked at his wife, his eyes touching her open blouse. Words slurred loosely when he spoke.

"Tramp. You're a tramp. You're no good, you're going to leave me, you were lying . . ."

Nora said quickly: "Shut up, Lyme."

Sam said nothing. The cabin seemed intolerably cramped. The girl wrenched free and stumbled aft into the open cockpit. Lyman lurched after her. Sam hesitated, feeling he had made a mistake somewhere. The sunlight was dazzling on the blue water of the cove.

"Lyme, you're drunk," he said. "Don't say anything you'll regret. I just came here to see you about the boatyard."

The big blond man swayed, trying to focus his blurred gaze. "Sam, I did you a big favor. Big favor, boy. I thought I stole your girl when I married Nora, and I figured myself for a heel. But I gave you a break, kid. I thought I could handle her, but you don't know what she is. Can't imagine, Sam. She eats men, she uses 'em . . ."

"Shut up," said Sam. "I don't want to hear it."

"I know you don't. I didn't, either. But when things like this slap you day after day, you wake up and face facts. Facts, Sam. But then it's too late to do anything. You're hooked. You've done things that can't be undone, see? And you can't get away from her after that."

Nora looked at Sam, smiling. "I'll handle him, darling. He's been like this for days. It's this cursed place. He needs help."

Abruptly Lyman Cameron sat down and covered his face with his hands. A sob came from between his taut fingers. His suit looked as if it had been slept in, his thick yellow hair was tangled and matted. Sam frowned. It wasn't like Lyman to let himself go like this. He looked at Nora, and she shook her head.

"Lyme, stop that noise." He felt deeply shocked, and the hatred for his brother was gone. "You're not acting like this because you found Nora and me here. It's something more than that. Nora says you're worried and frightened about something. What is it, Lyme?"

"Everything," the big man muttered. "I'm scared, yes."

"Of what?"

"I can't tell you."

"Who is the old man I brought in last night? What happened to him?"

"I don't know what you're talking about."

Sam said tightly: "Then I'm going to the cops with it. Nobody knows anything, but I picked up an old fellow at sea, half crazed by torture, and he disappears. Somebody slugs me, and when I ask about it, nobody knows anything. I'm fed up. It's a deal for the police, not for me."

Lyman took his hands from his face. Panic worked in his eyes. Nora still smiled, contempt on her face. Lyman stood up, staggering, and grabbed at the gunwale for support.

"Sam, it couldn't have happened better. Your coming here, I mean, in your boat. Nora and I are fed up here. What do you say, Sam? We can get away, all three of us, right now." He swung to Nora in appeal. "Let's not go back to the house, baby. Let's stay right here. We can get away in five minutes. Sam will take us, he'll do that for us. Then we'll be free of the whole rotten outfit."

Nora's face was white. Her voice cut like a whip.

"It's too late, you drunken fool."

"No, it's not! Sam . . ."

"Tell me what it's about," Sam said. "What are you both afraid of?"

Lyman said: "It's nothing."

Sam made an impatient sound and looked at Nora. He wondered what she was smiling about. Shaking her head, she looked at her blond husband. Lyman sobbed and then made a visible effort to pull himself together.

"All right, forget it," he said. "I feel better now."

Nora said: "You never were any good." Then her voice softened and she put her arm around Lyman. "Come along, darling. Casper will wonder what's keeping us."

Chapter Five

SAM SAT ON A BLUE FLAGSTONED PATIO AND watched Nate come out of Varden's house with a tray of highballs. He was beyond surprise. The big man shambled forward, as incongruous in these surroundings as the proverbial bull in a china shop. Nate's shaggy, sunburned torso was covered by a white mess jacket two sizes too small, although his shorts had been replaced by clean dungarees. Sam took a highball and said: "You get around, don't you?"

"So do you, matey. You like my dog?"

Sam looked across the patio at the Doberman Pinscher that strained at the end of his chain, striving to reach him. It was a fine, full-blooded animal, a vicious fighting machine.

"He doesn't go for strangers, does he?"

"Only to chew 'em up," Nate grinned. He shuffled away. Sam watched the dog lunge and fetch up short at the end of the chain. He settled back in the chair. It was an expensive chair, as expensive as the rest of Casper Varden's summer home. Only a man who had recently made a lot of money and wasn't used to it would build an English half-timbered house on an isolated rock off the coast of Maine. Everything was new, even the formal garden that edged the abrupt drop to the rocky surf below. Except for the beat of the surf, it was quiet here.

Sam tried the highball. His headache had returned, and the glare of light on the northern sea hurt his eyes, but he studied a long arc of breakers curving from the tip of Maquid Point. He looked at his watch and calculated that the tide would start ebbing in an hour. He frowned, thinking he had crossed that reef last night.

Behind him, a man chuckled. "You could walk half a mile out, if you knew the way, Mr. Cameron."

Sam didn't turn. "Pretty difficult, climbing over rock."

"It's mostly sand, Mr. Cameron. You might stub your toe here and there. I really wouldn't want to try it. There's only deep water at the end, anyway."

Casper Varden moved lightly around the chair and Sam stood up and shook hands with him. Varden didn't fit with Lyman's usual friends. The man was short and stocky, with thick black hair, pale and intelligent eyes behind straight-bowed glasses. His age was indeterminate, somewhere between thirty-five and forty. The Doberman growled as they shook hands. Varden's fingers were cold,

as limp and flexible as snakes. Smiling, he exhibited rather
bad teeth.

"Delighted, Sam. Lyman spoke of you often. It is un-
fortunate that he—ah, is feeling this way just now. But
Nora will take care of him. Devoted couple. They've done
much to brighten what otherwise would be a lonely vacation for me. I understand you've already met my step-
daughter, Ferne."

"Yes, I have."

"Very unlike Martha, her mother. Ferne is a strange
girl. She resents me because of her mother's death. She's
intelligent enough to know better. I hope you weren't too
badly impressed by what she must have said about us
here."

The man's words flowed over and around him while
Sam wondered if anyone had crossed the hump of the
headland from the south shore last night. Ferne or Eli
Broom, he thought.

"Have you had this place long?" he asked.

"I built the house two years ago. This is the first chance
I've had to spend time in it." Varden ducked his dark,
bookkeeper's head and sipped at the highball. "Nate is a
wizard with marine engines—he is overhauling my
schooner's auxiliary—but he was not born to be a house-
man. He's the only help I could get. Ferne, of course,
refused to live here. So we're roughing it, you might say.
You will stay with us, of course?"

"I haven't decided. In any case, I'd prefer to sleep on
my boat."

"As you wish, of course."

Sam sat down again and Varden walked over to the dog
and scratched its ears. The dog watched Sam. From the big
house behind them came the protest of Lyman's voice,
somewhere on the second floor. He couldn't hear Nora. A
muscle knotted along the ridge of his jaw. He finished the
highball and hoped it would end his headache. Casper
Varden lit a cigarette and offered one, which he refused.
The man was in a talkative mood.

"Maquid fascinated me the first time I saw it. History

is my hobby, and the darker the better. You've seen the monastery ruins on the hill?"

"I went through them," Sam said. "Last night."

"Oh?" But the man's voice was really without question. "Interesting ruins. But they need exploring. I've had no chance, as yet. The original monastery was built by a Jesuit explorer from Canada, in 1683. Father Dominique built a wooden retreat, which was promptly burned by the Indians. The next building lasted more than two centuries. Built of stone, you see. Local lore is full of fact and fancy, but I'm inclined to accept the statements that Dominique's Retreat was a hideout for Tories during the Revolution. The headland seems susceptible to disastrous fires, however. Less than fifty years ago, the structure was burned out and abandoned. The sea, the wind, and time itself played their parts in reducing those solid walls."

Sam said: "There have been other fires since."

"Oh, yes. During prohibition, Maquid was a good 'drop-off' for rum-runners coming from Canada. Smuggling played a part in the area's history, too. But in the late twenties, Maquid turned respectable. A man named Gorham built one of those white wooden hotels you see along the coast here and tried to develop a fashionable summer resort. He was successful for a time, until a fire swept the hotel and burned over half the woodland. Some lives were lost, I understand. Since then, my house is the only one to have been built here. I bought the north shore for a song, since local superstition in Haddamsport lowered the price. You see, I expect to go treasure-hunting here."

"Is there any treasure?" Sam asked.

Varden left the dog and sat on the terrace wall. He smiled. "I don't know. There might be a cache somewhere. There have been several expeditions by young hopefuls, but nothing was ever turned up. I really don't hope too much."

The man had run out of words. Sam looked back at the high crest of woodland behind the house. It wasn't more than a mile, straight across, to Ferne's place.

"Let's bring the history of Maquid up to date, shall

we?" he said. "For instance, I'd like last night to be explained."

Varden smiled, exhibiting his bad teeth again. "Ah, your old man of the sea, eh?"

"How did you know about him?"

"I could say that the wind has ears. But Nate told me about you, at breakfast. He was annoyed that Ferne helped you."

"Any reason for Nate to dislike me?"

Varden shrugged. "He hates the world."

"Who is the old man?" Sam insisted.

"I wish I knew. It is an intriguing yarn, Mr. Cameron. One would be inclined to credit it to your imagination, if your brother hadn't told me as much about you as he did. I'm sure there was an old man. But who he is, or what he was doing in that dory, I can't explain. Probably he's simply a local fisherman from Haddamsport who'd had too much to drink, and he came to after you landed and rowed himself home."

"And who slugged me after I came ashore? Someone watched me pick him up; I could see sunlight on binoculars for some time while I was still out to sea. Whoever watched me waited until I was deep in the woods on the way here, and tried to kill me."

"Surely you are exaggerating?"

Sam said: "I didn't fall down and go around in a state of self-induced shock, if that's what you mean."

"But it is possible. I'm sure there's no old man on Maquid."

"I'm not so sure. For one thing, he wasn't drunk. He had been tortured. His fingers were broken, his feet scorched, his ribs beaten in. He was half crazy with pain and fear. He couldn't have rowed that dory all the way to Haddamsport. He was more dead than alive when I left him."

Varden's pale eyes glinted oddly. "Incredible."

"I think," Sam said, "it's a matter for the police."

"If you insist," Varden nodded. He touched the broad bows of his glasses. "We have no telephone, of course. Nor is there a decent road to town except along the beaches. Our only real communication with Haddamsport is by way of the sea. The Panther is out of commission while Nate overhauls the engine, but we have the runabout. If you'd like to speak to the local authorities. . . ." Varden paused and smiled ruefully. "But I am afraid you wouldn't get help there. Your story doesn't make sense."

"We might find out if any fishermen are missing."

"True. On the other hand, my privacy would be invaded."

"Would you object to that?" Sam asked.

"Let us say that I would prefer to do my own searching." Varden's heavy jaw was stubborn. "I would regret any sensationalism in the press, although I have nothing to hide. Maquid provides me an escape from the world which would be destroyed by publicity. I must ask you to go slow, Mr. Cameron."

"But the old fellow may be dying somewhere."

"We will search for him ourselves."

Sam paused, feeling a cool prickle of danger. Varden had offered good advice in going slow. There was too much he didn't know. It would be easy to forget the whole matter, since last night's attack on him had evidently been declared a mistake. But there was a stubbornness in him that stiffened with each blank wall he met.

And there was Nora. He couldn't ignore her appeal for help. Then, remembering Ferne Dolson, his confusion deepened. He was sure she knew of the old man, but a blunt question would never get the truth out of her. He told himself this while he sat quietly, watching the dog and Casper Varden, and he knew that what really held him back was the latent danger of this place and this man. He had sailed into something he did not understand, except that its underlying threat was as sharply defined as the sunlight on the sea.

Casper Varden smiled again.

"You have decided to be considerate about the matter. I am grateful. You must consider yourself my guest for as long as you stay on Maquid. And now, if we can find Nathaniel, we will lunch and afterward consider searching for your old man of the sea."

Lyman did not come down for the meal, but Nora appeared, trim and cool in white slacks and a red, candy-striped silk blouse. She made excuses for Lyman and smiled almost impersonally at Sam. Looking at her, he had to struggle against the past. Fortunately, Varden kept the conversation on the local history, and Sam contented himself with only a few polite questions. Nate proved surprisingly adept as both cook and butler.

THE SUBJECT OF THE SEARCH WAS NOT RE-vived. Sam said nothing more about it. Promptly after lunch, Nora excused herself to look after Lyman, and Varden pleaded paper work to do. Sam found himself alone. He was not sorry for the respite. For twenty hours things had been piling up without an opportunity to sort them out. He left quietly, walking through the formal garden and along the path that skirted the northern beaches.

The air was clear, the sea placid and smooth. The reef was almost entirely exposed now. He looked back at the brooding house that might have served better as a stage setting for some Elizabethan tragedy. The mullioned windows shimmered blankly in the hot August sun. Smoke made a haze over the northern reaches of the coast, and he looked up at Maquid Hill, where the naked stone walls of Father Dominique's monastery stood in the stark sunlight. Nothing stirred anywhere. He walked on, crossing the line of unburned woodland that came down to the beach and entered the burned-over area. The wooden hotel that Varden had mentioned stood on the dunes in the center of a charred desolation.

Loneliness covered the place like a shroud. The hotel had not been entirely gutted; most of it stood, three stories high, with intricately fretted rails and balconies and rambling wings. The old yellow paint, blistered and scorched, still showed the black imprint of fire. Most of the roof was gone. Pausing, he looked at the long rows of shattered windows.

Something fluttered momentarily from one of the openings on the second floor. He started, then relaxed with a grimace as he saw it was only a rag of window curtain blowing in the sea wind. Nerves, he thought wryly. Turning, he retraced his steps and circled Varden's house again to reach the anchorage cove on the east side.

Varden's black-hulled schooner had turned with the tide, her narrow transom presented to him with its gilt lettering, *Panther, New York*, in fine italics. He admired her lines. A boat like that, he thought, could sail around the world comfortably.

He felt suddenly curious to learn more about her, and got into one of the dinghies where the Holiday lay and rowed out to the schooner, wondering who actually sailed her. Varden didn't seem much of a yachtsman, although there had been nothing to yield such a judgment. The better chance was that Lyman had handled the Panther on her trip north.

He brought the dinghy alongside the starboard quarter and climbed to the broad mahogany deck. Over-rigged, all right. But the best of materials and craftsmanship had gone into her, so that the brightwork and furled sails seemed almost new, the result of loving care. Fifteen minutes later, he knew a number of other things about the Panther that surprised him.

She was roomy below-deck. A quick survey of the main cabin and the two forward compartments revealed nothing unusual. The engine room, with its auxiliary power plant, bore out Varden's statement that Nate was overhauling the Diesel. The engine head had been removed and parts were scattered about among a litter of greasy tools. But it was the galley and store-room that puzzled him. The Panther had enough provisions aboard to remain at sea for months, with extra water tanks and fuel cans stowed in every available corner.

It was hot down here. He moved amidships, into the cabin that doubled as a salon and dining room. It was furnished in the same overelegant taste as the house, with walnut paneled bulkheads and soft leather curtains over the ports. There were framed photos on the walls, and Sam moved to the largest that hung over a built-in desk of curly maple. The photograph had been taken some years ago, when the Panther was painted white; but the lines of the schooner couldn't be mistaken. A canvas deck awning stretched aft, and under it a group of men in yachting clothes had posed. Sam felt a swift tingle of recognition. His attention focussed on the small man in the center of the group, and he whistled soundlessly. No mistake about it. Full-fleshed and tanned and smiling, the little man who had posed for that picture was the same wreck he had picked up, tortured and dying, at sea the day before.

It was a connection. He felt suddenly more sure of himself. His thoughts churned, trying to evaluate this new piece for his jigsaw puzzle, and he did not hear the second dinghy slide alongside the hull; he did not hear the soft, shuffling footsteps on deck, or the further sound of someone descending into the cabin behind him.

The first he knew of anyone else being aboard was when something struck him blindingly across the head. He crashed sidewise, slamming against the wall, and twisted about, almost on his knees. He looked up through a haze of pain and fury, and found himself staring into the twin muzzle of a twelve-gauge shotgun.

Behind the gun, Nate stood grinning down at him.

Chapter Six

NATE SAID: "GET UP AND GET OUT."

The fat man had reverted to his stained khaki shorts and naked, hairy chest. His bald head caught a highlight from the portholes. Under his shaggy brows, his small eyes were malevolent.

Sam slid upright with his shoulders pressed against the wall. He moved with care. He drew a deep breath against the pain and touched his right ear. There was a deep furrow in his scalp just above it, and his fingers came away wet with blood.

"You walk softly for a fat man, Nate," he said.

"But I got a heavy trigger finger. Get moving."

"I didn't know I was trespassing."

"You know it now."

"Nate," Sam said.

"Yeah?"

"What did you do with him last night?"

"With who?"

"Nate," Sam said. "I owe you something."

The shotgun prodded him. The metal felt cold and hard against the taut, retracting muscles of his stomach. Nate pressed harder. He grinned again. His face shone with sweat.

"You run off pretty loose at the mouth, for a guy with a gun in his gut."

Sam said: "I guess I just don't know any better. Maybe you knocked a few pins loose this time, Nate."

"It was a pleasure. Now do you get going, or do I do it again?"

"I'm going," Sam said.

He had difficulty getting up the ladder. He wanted to lie down on the warm deck and heave his stomach up until he died. The shotgun in his back allowed no such luxury. He could feel the blood run thick and slow behind his ear and down the side of his neck, and he let it run and didn't touch it again. The dinghy wobbled dangerously when he got into it. Nate leaned over the schooner's rail and shoved it away with his foot, and the surging motion made Sam fall forward over the thwart. He caught himself before he capsized the tiny eggshell and groped for the oars. He didn't look back. He heard Nate laugh and then he rowed slowly and painfully across the still, sunlit cove toward the Holiday. He tumbled headfirst into the sloop's cockpit and didn't move, unable to be sick, yet filled with an illness that was a combination of all the hate and rage and humiliation he had ever felt.

Presently he got up and moved forward into his cabin, searched for the canvas bucket and came back again to lower it over the side. He doused himself, and then filled it again. He stood there dripping, letting the cold water shock him back to his senses. Afterward he took off the wet dungarees borrowed from Ferne and spread them to dry on deck. The cut on his head had stopped bleeding, and was shallower than he had feared. He doctored himself the best he could and then took a fresh pair of white slacks from his gear and a striped basque shirt and a pair of dry sneakers. It was after four o'clock by then, and no one had come to the cove, although he had half expected Nora to follow him here. Nate had disappeared from the schooner, and so had his dinghy. The cove was empty and quiet. He wondered at everyone's absence, at the fact that he was being left alone to do pretty much as he pleased, even by Nora. There was a reason for it, he knew, but what it was seemed to escape him.

The wheezing of Ferne Dolson's lobster boat made him turn to the mouth of the cove. In a moment the Emma G. appeared, with Ferne at the tiller. Even from a distance, he could see she looked different. There was a blue ribbon in her hair, and her face had a freshly scrubbed look. A touch of lipstick gave a deeper color to her full mouth. More than that, she had discarded her working clothes and now wore a plaid skirt and blouse, with a wide leather belt around her slim waist.

Sam waited aboard the Holiday for her to come alongside.

"Did you see your friends?" she hailed him.

Her appearance may have changed for the better, but not her antagonism. He took the mooring line from her.

"What would you know about them?" he asked.

She tossed her dark hair. "Enough for me not to want to know them any better." Then her voice changed and held sympathy and alarm. "You've been hurt again!"

"It's getting to be a habit, lately."

"I don't understand it, Mr. Cameron." She stood there in her boat, shaking her head.

"Call me Sam," he said. "We know each other well enough, especially after last night. I've no secrets from you."

She flushed. "Don't get ideas, will you?"

"No ideas," he grinned. "I haven't been able to think

straight since I got here." He pointedly studied the graceful flare of her skirt. "Are you paying a social call here?"

She tightened her lips. "I'm heading for Haddamsport. I just came around to see if you were all right."

"Worried about me?"

"Not the way you imagine. You ought to see a doctor about that cut on your head."

"I'd like to see Nate about it even more. Some day when he doesn't have a shotgun, that is."

She stared. "Did Nate do that to you?"

"Nice fellow," Sam nodded.

"Whatever for?"

"I snooped, presumably, where I wasn't wanted."

She looked puzzled. It occurred to Sam that she was attractive, not in a blatantly pretty way, but with a fresh wholesomeness like a clean sea wind. He felt surprised, and then stepped into the lobster boat with her.

"If you don't object, I'll go to town, too, and see that doctor you mentioned."

"I don't mind company," Ferne said.

"What about for dinner?"

"Maybe."

"Then you haven't a date with someone else?"

"I have a date." She smiled. "But I might be free for dinner. Anything but lobster, Mr. Cameron."

"Sam," he said.

"All right, Sam."

The incoming tide had covered the reef at the tip of the headland. Ferne skirted it and turned southeasterly for the mainland. The sea was calm and smooth. Sam listened to the pulse of the engine, then settled himself in the stern opposite the girl. Her dark hair stirred in the breeze. The skirt and blouse emphasized the fine outlines of her figure. He knew from watching her that she enjoyed the sea and the handling of the boat, and for a moment he saw a wild, cold beauty in her, a restless frustration like an unfinished song.

He said: "It must be lonely here in the winter."

"I told you, I teach school in Haddamsport. I like it."

"Just you and Nate, on Maquid?"

She looked at him. "He doesn't bother me too much. Lately he's more obnoxious, since he went to work for your friend."

"Your step-father? He isn't my friend. I never met him before today." The headland dropped behind. They passed a small green dragger outward bound for the redfish grounds, and Ferne waved to the two men on her deck. Sam said: "Have you lived here all your life?"

"Except for four years at State Teachers. Mom died the summer I graduated. I came home to find Varden trying to take over everything. He was perfectly beastly."

"Why didn't you sell out?"

She shrugged. "Part of Maquid was left in Casper's name. But he'll never get the old house from me. It's my home."

"But still lonely," Sam said.

"I like it that way." Ferne faced him, her mouth a challenge. "Does that satisfy your curiosity?"

"Partly. What about Eli Broom?"

"What about him?"

"Is he really an insurance man?"

Ferne said: "Why shouldn't he be?"

"I don't know. I just wonder, that's all. For instance, I wonder what you were doing on Varden's side of the point last night, since you feud with him. It was convenient and lucky for me, though, and perhaps I shouldn't question it."

Ferne said: "I was following Nate."

"Why?"

"He's up to something, with your crowd of friends."

"I told you, they're not my friends."

She looked at him. "Not even Nora?"

He grinned. "O.K. Was Eli Broom with you last night?"

"No." She paused. "He's only interested in bass."

"You're sure of that?"

"If he has any other interests, they're not my business. He's a paying guest. That's all I know about him."

But not all I want to know, Sam thought. She was disturbed by his questions, and he didn't ask any more.

The sound of the motor filled the silence between them. They passed the first nun buoy in the channel to Haddamsport Harbor, and the fishing wharves opened to their view, with the tourists' waterfront restaurants, the artists with their easels, the summer people with their cameras and outlandish costumes presumed to blend with Haddamsport's "quaint" atmosphere. Ferne throttled down as they rounded a long pier spread with seine nets drying in the sun.

"You haven't asked me about the old man," Ferne said.

"I've been waiting for you to explain it," Sam said. "This morning you said he didn't exist. Then, when you dropped me off, you admitted I wasn't drunk, after all."

"He exists, all right. But he's probably dead by now."

"How do you know?"

"I had a look at him."

"When?"

"Just after you went ashore last night."

"What did you do with him?"

"Nothing. I thought he was dead."

"Did you know him?"

Ferne shook her head. "I never saw him before."

"You must have."

Her voice was sharp. "I'm not in the habit of lying!"

"All right. Take it easy. Better reverse if you don't want to run your boat down Main Street."

The Town Landing was dead ahead. Ferne angrily slammed into reverse gear and gunned the throttle. The Emma G. fought her own momentum and then bumped hard against the old rubber tires that served as fenders on the landing. Sam made the lines fast and offered his hand to help her ashore. She ignored him and jumped nimbly to the pier. Several fishermen repairing nets nearby grinned at her.

"Hi, Ferne. How's Nate been behaving?"

Ferne smiled at them all. "Everything is fine, boys."

"Just let us know if you need anything, kid."

"Thanks. I will."

Their eyes were curious, watching Sam. He followed

her quick footsteps and said: "I guess you're the town mascot."

"Everybody's had trouble with Nate. No one likes him."

"Then I've got plenty of company."

They climbed the steep sidewalk together into the upper part of town. Behind them, the harbor was dotted with pleasure craft and fishing boats. There were a few gift shops and cafés catering to the tourists, but for the most part Haddamsport led an independent life, making few concessions to the whims of visitors. He liked the looks of the town at once. Ferne turned another corner and paused at a big, barn-like sail loft.

"I've got some business here," she said. "There's only one doctor in town, but he's good. His name is McReadie. You'll find him on Lemon Street."

"And what about dinner?" Sam asked.

She hesitated. "In that salty outfit of yours, we'd better not try the Casino," she smiled. "It's for New Yorkers, mostly. Let's stick to Adam's Chop House. You'll find it on Main Street, just past Courthouse Square."

"In an hour?"

"I'll be there."

He watched her as she turned into the cavernous doorway of the loft, then retraced his steps and climbed uphill across Main Street. Dr. McReadie's house, pointed out by a passerby on Lemon Street, was white with black shutters, a fine Georgian doorway; its lawn was rich and green, the elm tree haughty and ancient, towering over the red brick chimney.

The doctor didn't stand on ceremony. He was a thin, spidery man with a high nasal twang and a glint of humor in his eyes.

"You've got a hard head, young man—harder than those of most of my customers. Still, I'd best fix you up, and then you take it easy for a few days. What was it—a waterfront brawl?"

"Something like that."

"Visitor to our fair town?"

"Just passing by."

"You need a shot of penicillin." Sam sat quietly in the cool shadows of the doctor's office, watching while the man sterilized a hypodermic. On the desk nearby was a framed photo of a young man—a thin-faced boy in a Navy officer's uniform. It was the same picture he'd seen in Ferne Dolson's house. He wondered if Ferne was in love with this young man, who looked to be Dr. McReadie's son. He said nothing about it. McReadie watched him in amused fashion.

"Was it a knife?"

"Eh? Oh, no." Sam paused. "A gun muzzle."

"What about the other fellow?" the doctor asked.

"He clobbered me," Sam said.

"Over a girl?"

Sam stood up. "You're damned curious, doctor."

McReadie chuckled. "I saw you come in the harbor in Ferne Dolson's boat. My back window has a fine view. The other fellow was Nate, I take it. Sit down, boy."

"You take it right," Sam said. "Let's have the needle." A few moments later, when he put on his shirt again, he said: "Judging from your questions, there isn't much that happens around here that you don't know about."

"Your guess is correct, and I am not offended. Seeing you're a friend of Ferne's, I'll charge you five dollars."

"Have any local fishermen been reported missing, the last day or two?"

Dr. McReadie didn't look up. He knocked on his wooden desk. "Haven't had a sea mishap in two months. If any dragger or seiner lost a man, I didn't hear about it. And I would have."

"I'm sure you would," Sam said. "Thanks very much."

"For the shot, or the information?"

"Both."

He had forty minutes before he was to meet Ferne at the restaurant. He wandered down Main Street and stopped at a bar where he had an ale and ate a pickled egg. There was a public telephone booth in a corner. He walked to it and closed himself in with several dollars in change, then began making long-distance calls. The trail led eventually to Hartford, Connecticut, and at the end of fifteen patient minutes, he learned that Mr. Eli Broom was not employed by any insurance company there. Sam thanked the anonymous voice and hung up. It didn't mean a thing.

He frowned and had another ale, thinking of Lyman and Casper Varden, of Eli Broom and Ferne. His uneasiness increased. The best thing to do was to go to the police. Whatever mess Lyman was in, the law was best for it. The old man's life was still at stake—assuming he was still alive. He closed his eyes, haunted by the mad fear in the old man's face. Lyman was mixed up in it, and Nora, too; or maybe Nora was only concerned with Lyman's welfare. His mouth twitched. Nora wanted silence from him, but she could have explained more to give him a basis to form a judgment of his own. Thinking of her, remembering her kiss, the feel of her mouth, he decided his main purpose here was still business. Somehow he had to get Lyman to sell his share of the boatyard. Strangely, he could think of Nora calmly, for the first time in a year, without emotional bias one way or the other. He grinned, wondering what had brought about the change. Then he mentally shook himself back to the issue at hand. He had twenty minutes to meet Ferne. Enough to walk to the courthouse and size up the law in Haddamsport.

The courthouse stood out in white, sharp clarity against the afternoon sunlight. He crossed the green, feeling relieved by his decision, and swung through the wide doors at the head of the stone steps, pausing for a moment in the cool, dim interior. A small, gilt-lettered sign over a door at the far end of the hall announced the office of the chief of police.

A woman stood waiting, halfway down the corridor. As she turned toward him his sense of free decision gave way to a sick plummeting of apprehension. It was Nora. She moved quietly, blocking his way to the chief's office.

"Sam."

Her bronze-colored hair shimmered as she tilted her head and looked up at him through dark lashes. Her mouth curved in a small, knowing smile.

"Sam," she said. "Don't go in there."

"It's the only thing to do." He felt stubborn. "I'm sorry, Nora."

"Sam, I asked you not to."

"But you didn't give me any reason."

"All right. I'll give you one. Maybe you'll go to the police anyway. It would be a simple solution, at that."

"What are you talking about?"

"I'm talking about your brother. If you go to the police, Lyman will hang for murder."

Chapter Seven

SAM THOUGHT: *SHE MEANS IT. SHE ISN'T LYING now.* It added up. It explained Lyman's panic, his desperate appeal to be taken from Maquid Point. He felt no surprise. It had been building up to that word all day. He had known it was coming. It was in the air.

"Murder." He said it aloud. "The old man, Nora?"

Her voice was quick. "Let's get out of here."

He looked at the door to the police chief's office and then yielded to the tug of her hand and followed her out to the sunlit courthouse steps. In the moment that had passed, no one had entered or seen them. The green looked the same. Two old men played chess on a stone bench near the Civil War Monument. A woman wheeled a baby carriage along the walk. Pigeons scattered as a passing car rumbled over the cobblestoned street, their wings whirring. Everything was the same, yet not the same. Anger filled him, and his voice was savage.

"What's Lyman done? What did he get into?"

"We can't talk here," Nora said.

"How did you know I'd come here? What made you wait?"

She smiled. "I know you, Sam. And I knew I hadn't persuaded you this morning. Varden was coming down

the shore anyway, and when I saw you leave Maquid wi..
Ferne Dolson, I decided to join him. I knew you couldn't
do anything else, darling." She touched his arm again.
"Come along. People will notice us."

"I don't care about people. I want to know about
Lyman." He paused suddenly. "You've found the old
man?"

"Not exactly."

"What do you mean, not exactly?"

"Sam, please."

"I want to know. I want a straight answer."

"Over there." She pointed across the street to the little
park. "Let's sit down first."

They walked past a party of tourists, a stout harassed
man with a sunburned face and two middle-aged women
in his wake. The chess players didn't look up as they went
by. Nora turned off on a path that led to the opposite
corner of the green, her steps oddly silent in her white
moccasins, unlike the quick, remembered click of her high
heels in Manhattan.

"This is good enough," Sam said. "Take this bench."

"All right, darling."

Her face was calm now. She fumbled for a cigarette and
handed Sam her gold lighter. He thumbed the wheel and
held the flame for her as she bent her head. Her shoulder
pressed against his, and then she straightened, her smile
telling him she remembered everything he remembered, the
you-and-me that once had been.

"Sam, darling."

His voice was a plea. "Level with me, Nora. I've got to
know where I stand in all this."

"You do love me, don't you, Sam?"

He didn't answer.

"Do you think I'm poison, as Lyman said?"

"I don't think about anything Lyman says. I'm thinking
of what you said. How will he hang for murder? Who did
he kill?"

"I'm not sure he killed anyone," Nora smiled.

"But you just said . . ."

"I had to stop you somehow, darling. It would be awful

if the police interfered now. I'm in trouble, too. Perhaps you, as well. Believe me, I know what's best for all of us, and the police would do nobody the least good."

"Tell me what you know."

"Right now?"

"Now."

She flicked her cigarette away. From the cannery on the waterfront came a high, prolonged whistle, ending the day's work. He watched Nora's mouth, saw her moisten her full underlip with the tip of her tongue. She shrugged.

"I don't know what it means," she said. "But perhaps in telling you, it may make sense. I didn't want to come here with Lyme in the first place. He insisted. He said he had a deal with Casper Varden, and he had to go." Nora's eyes were enormous with regret. "You don't know how we've lived, Lyman and I. He's not like you, Sam. He's not strong. He's always looking for the easy way, the quick way to make money. He saw a chance for easy money with Casper Varden."

"How?"

"That's what I don't know. Whatever it is, Lyman hasn't the nerve to go through with it. You saw how frightened he was this morning. I'm frightened, too. He's under Varden's thumb, and whatever the scheme is, Lyman is in too deep to pull out."

"What sort of scheme could it be?"

"I don't know."

"What about the old man? Has he been found yet?"

"I think he was on the Point when we arrived. He was living at the house. I never actually met him. I barely glimpsed him the day we came there, and then he—he just vanished."

"Until I returned him in my boat?"

"Yes."

He frowned. He thought she was lying. "But who is he? What did he do?"

"Lyman wouldn't say."

"Do you think Lyman killed him—at Varden's orders?"

"It's beyond me," Nora said. "If you won't help for

Lyman's sake, darling, you've got to help me. I'm in this, too!"

Sam said: "You're making yourself an accessory to murder. And if I keep it quiet, I'm in it, too."

"But we don't know it's murder yet, Sam!"

"It will be," he said. "I'm sure of it."

She made a gesture of despair. "What do you want me to do, Sam? What can I say? Maybe the police would be best—but they won't exonerate me. They'll think I've been in it from the start."

He sat still, aware that she had deftly switched sides somehow, after halting his decision to go to the police. Did she know that he couldn't do it now? He had no affection for Lyman; he and Lyman had never gotten along. And when Nora came between them with her smile, with her provocative body, that was the end of any normal fraternal relationship. Lyman ceased to exist as a brother and became an enemy, hated with double the fury he'd have for a stranger. And yet . . .

And yet, he thought, and knew that Nora had seen his grimace. A squirrel came bounding across the green, pausing to look and then scamper away. The shadows were long under the elms. Far off on the edge of the sea a thin overcast crept over the rim of the world. Sailing up here, he hadn't imagined anything like this. He had been full of Nora as she had been, alone with him, making love to him and asking for all he had in return.

Nora's voice, with its peculiar breathless quality, whispered again. "Whatever you do will be all right with me. I've always made mistakes, darling. It's not fair, but I'm leaving it to you to make things right for us again."

For us, he thought. She meant that if Lyman was gone, they would be free again to mend the fragments of his hungry dream. If he threw Lyman to the wolves—weak, handsome, arrogant Lyman—Nora would stand beside Sam and smile, as she smiled now.

He started to speak, not even sure of his answer, and then someone came walking swiftly down the path across the green. He felt Nora's quick start, and her shoulder withdrew from his and he looked up. It was Casper

en, like a squat, owl-eyed bulldog in his white flan-
els and blue yachting coat, his big jaw grim, his horn-
rimmed glasses catching the last of the sun in sharp splinters of light. He should have looked ludicrous, but there
was nothing funny about him, Sam thought, and he felt a
queer chill, waiting for Varden to reach their bench.

He propped himself before them, hips askew, leaning
on a gnarled walking stick heavily tipped with a gold
knob.

"Nora, did you know Lyman is in town?"

"But he couldn't be!"

"I saw him. He got away, and he looked like a crazy
man when he recognized me. He didn't give me a chance
to talk to him. I wanted to persuade him that his fears are
foolish. He's apt to do anything now. He must be stopped.
We must find him."

Nora stood up quickly. "Sam will help us."

Varden looked speculative. "Have you talked with your
brother, Mr. Cameron?"

"Only a little."

"Lyman is in serious difficulties. The nature of it is
unimportant at the moment, but his panic and flight may
create grave complications. He must be found and reasoned with."

"I'm with you that far," Sam said. "But where are you
going to look?"

"The railroad station," Nora said. "There's a train for
Portland in ten minutes. He'll try for that."

Varden swung his gold-knobbed stick. "Come along.
Hurry."

His urgency tolerated no further questions. Sam went
with them across the green. The chess players had folded
their board and gone home. The pigeons were roosting in
the courthouse tower.

The station was at the opposite end of town, just
touching the edge of the community among the rickety
shacks and shanties of seasonal fishermen. To the left,
gray-white dunes stretched away to the beach, overgrown
with coarse grass, with here and there the broad tracks of
a beach wagon making a trail through the waste. Inland,

the inevitable pine woods began, a wall of shadow a[g]
the orange evening sky. The station itself was a rambli[ng]
platform sheltered by a shingled cedar roof that had
turned gray in the salt air. A taxi and two private cars
were in the parking area, and on the platform were two
stout women and a young man in tennis shorts, his canvas
grips and rackets strapped together beside him.

Varden consulted his watch. "He may be in the waiting
room."

The station building smelled musty, with smooth wood-
en benches and the ticket agent's cage. The tin-shaded
lights were already turned on against the gathering shadows. No one was visible but the stationmaster. As they
entered, a door banged from the platform side of the
building and the taxi driver came in.

"He isn't here," Nora said.

Varden swung his cane. "He might have hired a car. Or
he might be in a bar, getting more drunk than usual."

"What's he running from?" Sam asked. "From you?"

Varden smiled tightly. "He is running from a crime he
committed. He is your brother, of course, but don't waste
any habitual loyalty on him. It's for the best that we find
him."

The train whistle sounded faintly through the pine
woods across the tracks, the sound echoing through the
narrow alleys of tumbledown shacks that paralleled the
rails. The stationmaster took off his green eyeshade and
came out of his cubicle, locking the door. His glance at
them was without curiosity.

"Train for Portland," he announced.

He went out and Nora, at a nod from Varden, followed. Varden said: "He may try to slip aboard at the last
moment. He must be somewhere nearby. You watch outside, and I'll cover this end."

Sam nodded and went out into the sandy parking lot.
The boy with the tennis rackets gathered them up and was
looking down the tracks for the train. The two women
were chatting rapidly, as if trying to rid themselves of
every conversational tidbit at the last moment. Turning,
he saw Nora's tall figure in her white dress. The ground

and the whistle sounded louder, and then the ancient locomotive rumbled into sight, hissing and snorting.
The train came to a halt. Sam looked at the shacks, then
at the sand dunes. He felt conflicting emotions, thinking of
Lyman with more pity than he had suspected. Turning
again, he saw one of the elderly ladies climb into the first of
the two wooden coaches. The athletic youth was already
aboard. Nora came rapidly back to the platform.

Sam heard Lyman's voice before he saw him. Surprisingly, it came from within the station, loud with alarm. He
turned, thinking that Lyman had been hidden in a rest
room all the time, then he broke into a run across the
parking lot. Lyman burst through the doorway before he
got there. He was wearing a disheveled white suit, his
yellow hair was rumpled, and he swung a large leather grip
in his left hand. With his right, he warded off Casper
Varden's grip. His face was desperate with panic.

"Don't let him get aboard!" Varden shouted.

Lyman saw Sam at that moment and plunged to the
right, then halted again as Nora blocked his way. The
sound of the conductor's starting bell came clearly above
the laborious, steamy breathing of the locomotive. Lyman
shouted, a sound that was broken by the scream of the
train whistle. He wasn't going to make it. He turned,
hampered by the leather grip, and tried to plunge around
Varden to get back on the platform and reach the train.
Varden slashed at him with his cane. The stick missed
Lyman's head and smashed down on his arm. Lyman
screamed in pain and reeled backward. The next moment
Sam reached them, aware of nothing but a wild, avenging
fury.

He blocked Varden's second blow with his hand,
catching at the man's wrist and twisting hard. The man
was shockingly strong. His fingers closed around Varden's
thick wrist and the heavy cane swished harmlessly aside.
Varden panted and wrenched free. His eyes were furious.
The sound of running footsteps made Sam turn, and he
saw that Lyman had taken advantage of his interference
to break free. But he wasn't running for the train. Nora
stood between him and the station. He was heading for a

shadowed alley between the shacks that edged roadbed.

The locomotive whistle sounded impatiently.

Varden panted: "You fool!"

Sam said: "Never mind. He didn't catch the train."

Lyman was staggering in the soft edge of sand that bordered the parking lot. He held his right arm at a peculiar angle, as if it were broken. And despite the hampering weight of his traveling bag, he didn't drop it. It swung in his left hand, throwing him off balance as he ran.

Varden cursed and ran after him. The stationmaster had crossed the platform by now, his mouth shouting unintelligible questions. The train rumbled out of the station. In the doorway, the taxi driver chewed his cigar and looked on, not interfering.

Sam turned away, his anger fading. Oddly, he remembered a long series of boyhood fights along the waterfronts of the North Shore, fights he had forgotten until now. Always it had been Lyman who got into trouble, and always Sam had to pitch in to rescue him. It was as if time had turned backward for a moment, and he felt again his earlier loyalty toward a troublesome brother. There was something to blood being thicker than water, he reflected, regardless of what Lyman had done to him in the past. It wasn't in him to stand idly by and see Lyman, in panicky flight, subdued by the cold brutality of Varden's lead-weighted cane. No matter what Lyman had done, no matter what Lyman would do in the future.

The stationmaster tugged at his arm, asking questions. Sam shook him off and followed Varden into the alley. Lyman had vanished, still hanging on to the bag. Sam didn't think Varden would catch up to him: not this time, anyway. He tried to think of what Lyman would do now, in his effort to get out of Haddamsport. Rent a car, perhaps. There were two or three garages in town where he might hire one. Then he remembered the curious twist to Lyman's right arm. He was sure Varden had broken it with his cane. If that were so, then Lyman couldn't drive. He was trapped in Haddamsport.

..ra came walking down the alley between the shan-
..es. Her face was white. She looked at Sam as if he were a
stranger.

"He got away," she said bluntly. "Why did you help
him?"

"I don't know," Sam said.

Varden's stocky figure appeared in the alley. The man's
horn-rimmed glasses were askew, and he adjusted them,
the shimmering lenses masking his eyes in the dim light.
His voice was normal when he spoke, a bit resigned.

"He'll probably make for the waterfront now. I don't
know how he got ashore here at all, but he'll realize it was
a mistake and try to get away by sea. We must catch him
and reason with him, for his own good as well as for our
own safety. I know you do not understand much of this,
Mr. Cameron, but you will. You will, indeed."

"That's a fine stick you have there," Sam said.

"It is useful."

"Did you break his arm?"

"I may have. I think so."

Sam said: "For his own good, no doubt."

Varden shrugged. "There is no point in staying here.
The next train doesn't leave for more than two hours. I
think, Mr. Cameron, in view of your attitude, that we had
best part right here."

Sam looked at Nora. "Are you going with him?"

She hesitated. "I think I'd better."

"Happy hunting, then," Sam said.

He walked away, down the alley that opened into a
small street that angled toward Haddamsport center. He
had no particular destination in mind. The whole evening
sky was overcast now, and darkness came on prematurely.
The tangled masts of fishing boats in the harbor made a
dark web against the water. Beyond the stone breakwater
at the harbor entrance, a flashing buoy sent pinpoints of
yellow light across the channel.

He paused at the Mariner's Club on Front Street and
stood at the bar for a drink. He felt he needed it. Then, on
sudden impulse, he went upstairs to the club-room and
consulted the yacht registry there. No one paid any atten-

tion to him. The only people in the room were fis
captains playing cards at a round table near the window.
He flipped the pages of the book and ran his finger down
the list of names until he came to the Panther, registered
in New York. Buried in the small type describing the
schooner and her age was the name of her owner.

Amos V. Butterick.

He stood still, the shock of his discovery dissolving the
glow of liquor inside him. Butterick, again. He hadn't
connected the events here at Maquid Point with Nora's
past, with her so-called "benefactor" whom he had never
seen or met. Amos Butterick's name hadn't been mentioned by anyone. But there was a connection. It seemed
incredible that Nora, married now to Lyman, could still
be accepting favors from Butterick. Yet it had to be
something like that.

He wondered if Casper Varden could be the mysterious
millionaire, and dismissed the thought promptly.

He went to the window, near the card-playing fishing
captains, and watched the dark harbor. Near the
breakwater, the riding lights of a small boat made slow
progress, outward bound. It was a lobster boat.

Sam looked at his watch with dismay.

It was an hour past the time he had promised to meet
Ferne Dolson for dinner. He had forgotten.

Chapter Eight

ADAM'S CHOP HOUSE ON MAIN STREET HAD
oak-paneled walls and a steamy atmosphere generated by
cooking clams and seafood. There were a few tourists at
tables among the wooden booths, but the bulk of the
customers appeared to be native fishermen. Sam pushed
open the screen door and deliberately let it slam behind
him. Two or three of the diners glanced up at him and

then returned to their meals. At a far table in a corner, Ferne Dolson watched him over the rim of her coffee cup. Eli Broom was with her.

He grinned and started toward them, and Ferne put down her cup and watched him with angry eyes. The dark-haired girl said something to Eli Broom, and he turned to observe Sam's approach, too. The thin, boyish-looking man pushed back his wheat-colored hair and said:

"Your loss is my gain, Mr. Cameron. You look better than you did this morning."

"Thanks. . . . I'm sorry, Ferne. I got tied up."

Ferne said: "I know. I saw you with her."

"May I sit down?"

"We're just finished," Ferne said. Her voice was cold.

He pulled out a chair and seated himself anyway. Ferne didn't look at him. She studied her coffee cup and then said: "Come on, Eli. Let's go home."

"Wait a minute." Sam put a hand on her arm. "I told you I was sorry. What's biting you, anyway? Do you always have to carry a chip on your shoulder?"

Eli Broom laughed softly. "You're being jealous, Ferne. You give yourself away, that way. Just because Mr. Cameron met his sister-in-law and was delayed is no reason to treat him like a leper."

Ferne's mouth curled. "I saw him. He's in love with her." A dull flush crept up her cheeks and she pulled her arm from Sam's hand. "It's none of my business. I don't like to be stood up, that's all."

"I'm here," Sam said. "I'm late, but I'm here."

Her eyes glared dangerously, but she said nothing. A waiter came over, wiping his hands on a damp apron, and Sam ordered fried clams and coffee. The waiter looked at Eli Broom, and the slim man said, "Nothing more, thanks." The waiter went away. Broom took cigarettes from his coat pocket and offered them, his thin student's face perfectly open and friendly. Sam wondered whether he should question him about his alleged employment in the insurance business, and then decided that this was hardly the time. The fact that Broom was ashore in Haddamsport, together with everyone else from Maquid Point, might be significant. The man was mixed up in this, too, he decided. But direct questions would get him nowhere.

Ferne spoke suddenly with forced calm. "Mr. Broom likes to tease, Sam. Don't get ideas from anything he said."

"I won't," Sam promised.

"Shall we go now, Eli?"

Broom said: "Maybe Mr. Cameron would like a lift back to Maquid."

"Thanks, but I'm not ready to go back yet," Sam said.

He stood up as Ferne rose, and Eli Broom followed her out of the restaurant. The waiter arrived with his clams and coffee, and said: "That Ferne. Cute trick. First time I ever seen her do that."

"Do what?"

"Crying in her coffee cup, just before you came in. The guy had a time with her, all right. They were talking, and then she up and slapped him in the face and busted into tears. That ain't like Ferne Dolson."

"You know her pretty well?" Sam asked.

"Everybody knows Ferne. Nice kid."

"What about her stepfather, Mr. Varden?"

"He's snooty. He ain't here much."

"And Nate?"

"That son of a bitch," the waiter said.

He went away. Sam ate quickly, startled to find himself thinking of Ferne in terms of chagrin. He must have been pretty obvious, sitting there in the park with Nora, looking like a love-sick calf. What was the matter with him, anyway? His confused emotions made no sense at all. Everything had revolved around Nora for so long that he had lost perspective. He felt mixed up, and somewhere in the welter of his thoughts was Ferne Dolson.

Deliberately he forced himself to think in terms of Lyman's troubles. Everything else was a side issue. If he could find Lyman before Varden did, he'd have a chance to make him talk. Lyman was into something over his head, driven to desperate flight. It might not yet be murder, Sam decided, but it would be, unless it were stopped.

Lyman was the key to his future steps. He had to be found.

He finished his coffee, paid his check, and went to the street again, trying to decide where Lyman could be. Lyman wanted to get out of town, but having been stopped at the railroad station once, he wouldn't be likely to try that again. There were boats, of course, as well as passing cars that might give him a lift down the coast. There was no point in trying to cover the town alone. He knew Lyman better than anyone else involved, knew what Lyman was most apt to do under any set of circumstances.

It came to him that Lyman wouldn't do anything before taking care of his injured arm. Not even panic could overcome his chronic hypochondria that Sam remembered from their childhood days. He turned the corner, quickening his pace. It was as good a guess as any, and far better than aimlessly scouring the town. The sidewalks were getting crowded, now that the dinner hour was past, and he bucked through the tourists on Main Street and continued on up to the corner of Lemon. The town lights were on, and the lamp on the corner shed a dull yellow glow on the smooth lawn and the fine old colonial house under the elms. An electric sign, small and discreet, announced this as Dr. McReadie's residence.

Dr. McReadie, according to Ferne, was the only medical man in town. Lyman had to come here—perhaps had already come and gone.

The sound of traffic on Main Street seemed remote as he turned up the walk and mounted the porch steps. A light shone far back in the house, dimly visible through the curtained glass of the front door. He found the ancient contraption of polished brass, pulled on it and listened to it peal somewhere within. Standing there, hoping that the talkative doctor was at home, he suddenly felt the importance of finding Lyman first and talking things out with him. He had been groping in the dark too long, and only Lyman could give him the answers he needed. He was glad now that Nora had intercepted him on the way to the police. He owed it to Lyman to get the facts before he made any irrevocable moves.

The glass paneled door opened before him.

"Yes, young man?"

A small dumpling of a woman stood peering out at him.

"Is Dr. McReadie in?"

"Visiting hours are from three to five in the afternoon. Unless it's an emergency . . ."

"It is," Sam said.

"Well . . . Come in, please."

The stout little woman bustled down the dark hallway to the rear of the house. Sam followed, his sneakers making no sound on the runner. He passed the door that opened into the doctor's office, as he knew from his earlier visit that afternoon. The woman showed him into a small sitting room.

"Be seated, please. I'll tell the doctor he's wanted."

The house resumed its silence when the woman vanished. Sam selected a leather armchair and stared at a tall, glass-encased set of book shelves against the opposite wall. The wall was paneled, which reminded him of the cabin aboard the Panther, and the photo he had seen there of the nameless old man. He wondered if Nate's savage attack had been stimulated by the fact that he had been caught studying the photograph, and then he was interrupted by the entrance of Dr. McReadie.

"Ah, Mr. Cameron. I hoped to see you again."

He started to rise and was waved back by the doctor's gaunt hand. McReadie took another seat across the room and settled himself in it with care, as if his spidery frame was excessively fragile. The man's long, bony face looked pleased.

"You're feeling all right? No after-effects?"

"I feel fine," Sam said. "But I'm worried about my brother."

"Oh? You mean Lyman?"

His voice quickened. "That's right. Was he here?"

"Twenty minutes ago. Very interesting, really. You as much as accused me of being the town gossip, young man, but I am sure you will understand my curiosity about you two. Was it your brother you fought with?"

"No."

"I didn't think so. He was in a highly hysterical state. Would it be too much if you told me what this is all about?"

"I don't know myself."

"Nonsense. Of course you do."

"Did Lyman say where he was going when he left here?"

"To the hospital, I hope. I couldn't do much for his arm, except to make a preliminary examination. He wouldn't let me."

"His arm was broken?"

"Rather severely."

Twenty minutes, Sam thought. The time he had spent with Ferne and Eli Broom, in the restaurant. If he'd thought of this in the first place, he could have intercepted Lyman here.

"Incidentally," Dr. McReadie said, "in talking with your brother, I mentioned your previous visit to me. He seemed deeply relieved that I knew you. He was incoherent, for the most part, and refused to take any sedative beyond a morphine tablet, but he was particularly lucid in reference to his instructions about you."

"What did he say about me?"

"He wanted me to find you. He had a traveling bag with him, and he was anxious for me to find you and turn it over to you."

"Do you have the bag now?" Sam asked.

"He left it with me, yes."

"All right," Sam said. "Where is it?"

The doctor sighed and smiled. "You're so direct. You won't satisfy my curiosity?"

"Later, if I can, I'll let you know what it's all about. I'm grateful for your help, Doctor. Where is the bag?"

McReadie said: "Behind the chair you're sitting in."

Sam got up and walked around it. The bag was there, all right. It was the same tan traveling grip that Lyman had seemed so reluctant to lose. He hadn't thought much about it before. Now the bag suddenly assumed an importance he hadn't suspected. He picked it up and put it on the chair, knowing that McReadie watched him with a strange eagerness.

"Have you opened it?" Sam asked.

"No. I was tempted, but I didn't."

"It's just an ordinary traveling bag," Sam said.

"Of course."

It was not just an ordinary bag. He was sure of it. So was the doctor. The man's avid curiosity was stamped in every line of his gaunt face. Quite suddenly, Sam knew that the man had examined the contents and was waiting for his own reaction, when he opened it. There was no point in further delay.

"All right," he muttered. "Let's have a look."

He put the bag on its side and loosened the buckles and threw back the tan cowhide straps. There was an ordinary brass lock that held down the lid, but it wasn't locked, and it snicked open when he thumbed the button that held the catch.

Sam lifted the lid, looked inside, and quickly shut it again.

He stood very still, his back to the doctor.

It was not too much of a shock. The grip was full of money, paper currency in neat packets, crammed into the bag until it all but overflowed. It was no small amount, either. The topmost bills of each packet were hundreds. There could be several hundreds of thousands there. He had no idea what the total would amount to. Where it had come from, though, and what he should do with it didn't matter at the moment. He hoped he'd been wrong in guessing that Dr. McReadie had already opened the bag.

He had not been wrong.

The doctor's voice was cool and amused when he spoke.

"Surprised, Mr. Cameron? Turn around. I have another surprise for you."

Sam turned slowly and looked at the gaunt man. McReadie still sat in the chair across the room, his thin

shoulders outlined by the light from a student lamp behind him. There was one difference, however. The doctor
had a gun in his hand, and the gun was pointed at Sam.

Chapter Nine

SAM SAID: "BE CAREFUL WITH THAT THING."

"I shall be. I regret this show of violence, I assure you.
I am a peaceful man. On the other hand, that is an
enormous sum of money in that bag."

"It doesn't belong to you," Sam said.

"Nor to you either." Dr. McReadie's voice trembled a
bit. The gun in his gnarled, liver-spotted hand trembled,
too. "I was curious about your reaction when you opened
that bag. You didn't know what was in it, did you?"

"No."

"Do you know where your brother got this money?"

"No."

"You don't know much, do you, Mr. Cameron?"

"No."

"I strongly suspect that one might label this money in the
category of 'finders keepers.' "

Sam said: "Let's take it to the cops."

"Oh, come now, Mr. Cameron!"

"Well, what do you suggest?"

"I am waiting for you to tell me about this money, and
where your brother got it."

"Then what?"

"Then we shall decide what to do with it. It is a great
amount of money. More than I ever hoped to see in all
my life. And I've had a long life, Mr. Cameron. One of
hard work, diligent labor, and acute boredom."

"But you've been honest," Sam said.

"Up to now, yes."

"Stay that way. Let's take it to the police."

"The sight of all this money doesn't affect you in any way?"

"That gun in your hand bothers me more. For all I know, it may be just a lot of worthless paper in that bag. It might be counterfeit."

Dr. McReadie frowned. "I hadn't thought of that."

"Well, think about it, and put your gun away and act sensibly," Sam said.

"I examined that currency rather carefully. I don't think you are right about its being counterfeit."

"Right or wrong, your thinking is screwy if you imagine you can get away with this money. You don't know where it came from, you don't know who's mixed up in it, you don't know who may come after it. Do you seriously think you'll be able to keep it?"

"I am going to try," McReadie said.

Sam was silent. He had the strong feeling that none of this was real, that the whole thing belonged in some nightmare world he had dreamed up. But the gun in Dr. McReadie's hand was real. And if a man like McReadie could throw aside a lifetime of conforming to accepted codes and ethics, then anything could happen. It was the money, of course. There was too much of it for most men to keep their balance when confronted with it. If there'd been less of it, then the doctor would certainly have called the police. As it was, McReadie had suddenly resolved to stick his finger into the pie. It didn't matter any longer who really owned the money. It was here, and it apparently worked its own spell on whoever saw it. Even within himself, he felt an odd stirring of possession, a reluctance to let it go.

He knew McReadie was watching him, over-excited, uncertain. His own mind raced along with the problem that seemed for the moment like a stalemate. But McReadie had the gun, and the gun could spell the difference between life and death.

And McReadie was talkative.

"It is a strange thing," he said, "what the sight of a fortune can do to a man. Here I've gone along for thirty years of my life, tending to the aches, sniffles and complaints of all of Haddamsport, hibernating in the winter and envying the tourists in the summer. Like everyone else, I once had hopes of ultimate success, dreaming a sort of vague dream fantasy of golden days to come. I had already given up that dream before you visited me today. And now here it is again, the means, the road to everything that life has denied me. I am not surprised at myself. I have little or nothing to lose by keeping this money."

"Only your life, perhaps," Sam said.

"And what is that worth, even to me?" Dr. McReadie handled the gun nervously. "I suspect you've been more truthful with me than not. I would like to propose a partnership."

"I'm listening."

"You are young and strong. You are resourceful. We can get away with this money, can't we?"

"Are you asking my opinion?"

"Yes. And your aid."

"The answer is no," Sam said. "If you want the money that badly, you can have it. All of it. I have other things to do, and I can't sit around here debating it with you. I'm leaving."

"Where will you go?"

"That's my business."

"But you may go to the police."

"Maybe," Sam said.

Dr. McReadie looked puzzled. It came to Sam that the man was deeply frightened, yet not without a certain desperate courage, too. It was quiet in the little sitting room. He wondered where the stout woman had gone, and whether she knew what was happening in here and was listening beyond the closed door. That would complicate matters, as if they needed any further complication.

"You don't think," McReadie asked again, "that we can get away with this money?"

"I know *you* can't," Sam said pointedly. "Lyman was pretty desperate to keep it, even with his broken arm. Why did he leave it here for me?"

"He saw someone watching the house, from the street."

"Who was it?"

"I don't know. I didn't see anyone. But it was then that he decided to leave the bag here. He made me let him out of the house by the back way."

"Then this place is already spotted," Sam said. "You won't get anywhere."

Turning, he picked up the grip, ignoring the gun in Dr. McReadie's hand. "I'm sorry to spoil that dream of yours, Doctor. I can imagine how you feel. I'm taking the money with me. I don't know whose it is, or where it came from; but I intend to find out. If there's a reward for its recovery, or even if it should be free booty, I won't forget you. You can count on that."

McReadie lurched up. His face was shiny with sweat. His shadow fell long and gaunt across the room. The lamplight ran a bright finger along the barrel of his gun.

"You are a brave but foolish young man. Even if you took the money, I could call the police and have you stopped."

Sam shrugged. "That's your privilege."

He started toward the door. McReadie made a curious gasping sound. His hand jerked, bringing up the gun. "Stop!"

Sam paused with his hand on the doorknob. "That would be murder, Doctor. I don't think that a man who has spent his life in your profession will fire that gun. Particularly when you won't gain anything, and have everything to lose."

"How can I trust you?" the man gasped. "How do I know you'll come back?"

"You don't. But I will."

"Suppose—suppose someone comes here and asks about your brother and the money?"

"Tell them I have it," Sam said.

He opened the door. The hall beyond was empty, dimly lighted from the back of the house. Behind him, he heard a click as Dr. McReadie dropped the revolver on the table. He didn't look back. He moved soundlessly toward the front door, holding the heavy grip in his left hand. The pudgy woman didn't appear. McReadie didn't follow.

ιe opened the double-leafed door a crack, and looked out into the tree-shadowed street. There was no one in sight. If anybody were watching the house, he was well hidden. He opened the door all the way and crossed the porch quickly and ran down the steps and over the lawn to the sidewalk. Nothing happened. He turned and walked at a slower pace down the hill toward Main Street.

The doctor might have recovered enough to be calling the police even now, but it didn't matter, Sam thought, if he moved fast enough. He was in it up to his neck now, and finding Lyman was more important than anything else. There was fear inside him, and reaction from his bluff with the doctor's gun. If he hadn't correctly sized up the doctor's inherent cowardice and greed, he'd never have left that house alive. There was nothing to do but continue playing his hunch on the doctor. He didn't think McReadie would call the police. Not yet, anyway.

No one paid any attention to him when he crossed Main Street and headed for the waterfront. Somewhere in the crowds on the sidewalk was Casper Varden. Nora, too. But he saw no one familiar, and in another moment he left the lighted thoroughfare and crossed into the shadows of darkened sail lofts, marine supply stores, and dilapidated frame buildings whose businesses were their own.

He passed a bar and then crossed the cobblestoned area of the Town Landing. The suitcase seemed heavier, and he shifted it to his right hand. The brick cannery loomed to his left, and beyond, the dark, stubby masts of fishing draggers stood out in a dim web against the harbor water. Far out to sea, a light winked dimly, once, then twice, and then went out. The sound of radio music came from the long white shape of a motor cruiser moored nearby, but there were no lights aboard. Sam picked his way across the uneven planks of the wharf, ducking between net spindles, and then paused at the stringpiece, looking down at the Holiday.

Lyman must have sailed her here from Maquid Point, Sam thought, which posed another facet to the problem. In the Holiday, Lyman could have headed out to sea and lost himself with the money, putting in at any of a dozen small harbors either up or down the Maine shore. Varden would have been hard put to get on his trail again; at the very least, Varden would have been seriously delayed. Sam frowned, studying the sails that spilled over the foredeck and the cockpit. The Holiday had been moored in a hurry, with no effort to care for her equipment, and that was unlike Lyman, too; but then, Lyman hadn't been himself. Perhaps there would never be any adequate accounting of Lyman's reasons for doing what he had done.

He went down the ladder carefully and swung the grip aboard to a seat in the cockpit. The sloop heeled with his weight and the mooring lines creaked. The tide slapped restlessly against the barnacled pilings of the wharf. He straightened and looked toward the spot where Ferne Dolson had moored her lobster boat. It was still there, tied to the same wharf, about fifty feet away. In the darkness, he couldn't tell if anyone was aboard. Then something white moved at her stern and Sam pushed the suitcase under the overflow of canvas that spilled down from the boom and went back up the ladder again to walk down the wharf toward the other boat.

Ferne was aboard. She acknowledged his presence without sound, only turning her head to watch him as he moved toward her. She was alone, and he wondered where Eli Broom could be. Her face was a pale mask in the gloom, he thought, turning toward him like a dream image created by the soft pattern of music coming from the darkened yacht moored nearby.

"I thought you'd be gone by now," he said.

"I'm waiting for Eli."

"Anyone else around?"

"I just got here."

There was a wall between them, created by her hostility—and her fear. She was afraid of him. Sam realized it with an inner shock, and knew further that he didn't want her to fear him, that he wanted her trust and confidence.

"I'm sorry about the dinner, Ferne," he said.

"It didn't matter. Don't make mountains out of molehills."

's more than just the dinner. What are you afraid
of?"

"I'm not afraid."

He watched her slight figure move away from him,
crowding into a corner of the stern. He wanted to touch
her, to reassure her, but he made no move toward her.
"Coming over here this evening, you started to tell me
something of what this was all about. Can't you tell me
more?"

"What did Nora tell you?"

"Nothing, except that my brother is in trouble. I know
that now, anyway. I want to help him. I didn't think I'd
feel this way, because we've had a lot of difficulties between us, but that's changed now."

"Your difficulty was Nora," Ferne said coldly.

"Yes, it was."

"Why should I help you?"

"Maybe because you'll be helping yourself, too," Sam
told her. "You know I'm no friend of Varden's."

"I'm not so sure. Eli Broom says you're just what you
claim to be; he said you didn't know what was going on,
and that the best thing you could do would be to pull out
of here before you got involved. But you're involved already, aren't you? Nora saw to that."

"Why do you hate her?"

"She doesn't mean anything to me, one way or another."

"Then why drag her into everything I say?"

"Because she's behind everything you've said and done
since you came here." Ferne turned toward him suddenly,
her dark eyes luminous in the shadows. "I suppose you
think I'm a fool. I know I haven't been anywhere or done
much of anything, and I don't pretend to know what
motivates people like you and Cas Varden and the others.
When I learned you were a boat designer, I thought you
loved the sea as I do, and therefore your arrival at
Maquid was just a coincidence of timing, an accident."

"It was," Sam said. "I walked into a hornets' nest."

"Well, you can walk right out of it again. You'll get no
help from me."

"Ferne . . ."

"Go away," she said. "Get off my boat."

He wanted to shake the stubborn temper out of her. But he didn't touch her and he didn't argue further. He got up and quit the Emma G., returning to the wharf. Someone, a woman, laughed aboard the darkened motor cruiser nearby, and the sound of laughter seemed unnecessarily loud, carried across the water. He walked back to the Holiday, feeling futile and helpless, looking down on the tumbled sails that littered her deck. Climbing aboard, he made sure the money bag was where he'd left it, and then hauled the canvas aside to give himself access to the cabin. He picked up the bag, wondering where he could conceal it, and decided to slide it under the bunk in the built-in luggage compartment as a temporary measure. Holding the money was like holding an ace in the hole. It would make the others come to him, and when they did, he would get the truth out of them, beginning with the mystery of the tortured old man.

The cabin was in inky darkness, but he needed no light to find his way about. His free hand slid along the cabinet doors on the port side, touched the cool smooth surface of the galley stove, and then found the upright of the bunk. He paused as a boat passed nearby, thinking it was Ferne leaving in the Emma G. But the engine didn't sound the same. The Holiday lifted and fell in the wash of the other vessel's wake, and he dropped to one knee and slid the heavy suitcase in behind his other bags under the bunk.

It was then that he knew he was not alone in the cabin.

Someone lay on the bunk, not moving, not breathing. The roll of the Holiday in the wake of the other boat had shifted a weight ever so slightly, and the hard springs creaked. Sam froze where he was, on one knee, beside the bunk.

A moment passed. And another. Nothing happened.

He straightened and reached out and touched a cool hand that dangled limply over the edge of the bunk. A man's hand. There was no life in it. He knew that instantly, without question, before the shock of the knowledge numbed him as he stood there. He didn't think of the

~~ger~~ as he reached overhead and snapped on the battery lamp.

The tiny cabin sprang into bright existence, and Sam stood looking down at the man who sprawled on the bunk. His search was over. It was his brother, Lyman.

A garish red stain was like an evil blot on Lyman's white linen coat. From the center of it stuck the wooden handle of a knife, and Sam looked at the knife with dull eyes, recognizing it as one from the sloop's galley, one of his own. He didn't touch it. He didn't touch Lyman. Lyman was beyond help now, because he was dead.

Chapter Ten

ANGER GREW SLOWLY WITHIN HIM, DEEP AND ruthless and implacable, spreading through his chest and up in his throat until he couldn't breathe. He forced himself to unclench his fists and flex his fingers. Whatever Lyman had done, whoever he had hurt, he didn't deserve this. No man deserved to die like this. A vast pity mingled with his anger, and a knowledge that what Lyman had done, in petty malice or greed, had not been viciously directed at himself. Lyman hadn't hated him. He had appealed for help, and Sam hadn't given him the help he needed.

Somewhere out in the harbor a boat's whistle sounded. Sam stared down at the dead man, not moving. The tiny cabin suddenly seemed cramped and unreal. Another boat passed, and again the Holiday rolled in its wake, and the dead man's dangling hand slid back and forth over the edge of the bunk. Sam lifted it and placed it at rest inside the wooden rail. Looking at his brother, he knew that a time had passed that was gone forever from his life. His thoughts churned on to other things, to questions that sprang unbidden in the back of his mind. Had McReadie known Lyman was dead? And Ferne? He remembered the strained, taut quality of her voice as he had left sitting in her boat not fifty feet away. She hadn't mentioned seeing Lyman, but she could have known that his cabin was occupied by the dead man. It fitted her behavior. He thought of Nora, and then of Casper Varden, and he wondered if this was the end of Varden's pursuit.

Under his feet, the sloop rolled once more, ever so slightly. No boat had passed this time. His hand shot up, reaching for the light switch. The cabin was plunged into darkness. He stood still, his hand upraised, not wanting to give himself away, and then knowing that it was too late already. Someone had come aboard. Someone was speaking to him from the open door of the cabin.

"Come out of there, Cameron."

It was Eli Broom. The slim, straw-haired man looked bigger, somehow, more competent, sure of himself, his lithe figure outlined against the faint glow in the sky behind him.

"Come out," he repeated.

Sam shrugged. He moved slowly, guessing that Broom's authority sprang from the fact that he was armed. He was right. The man held a service .45, and he held it competently, not like Dr. McReadie had done. He held it steadily, and he wasn't frightened, like the greedy doctor. He knew what he was doing.

"I'm coming," Sam said.

"Don't try anything."

Broom stepped back into the cockpit to allow Sam to get out of the cabin. The man smiled faintly. His voice was soft. Sam looked for Ferne, but she wasn't there. He wondered if she had sent Broom over here, or whether Broom had been waiting all this time, hidden in the shadows of the wharf nearby. It didn't matter.

"Take it easy," Sam said.

Broom nodded. "I pegged you wrong, Cameron. You finally up and did it, didn't you?"

"You've seen my brother?"

"Enough of him so that I know he's dead." There was a subtle change in the man's voice, an authority that went beyond the gun he carried. "I guessed wrong about you. I didn't think you were mixed up in this."

"I wasn't," Sam said, "until I came ashore here."

"But now you've killed him."

"No. I didn't do it."

"You'd say that anyway. If not you, who else did it?"

"I don't know. Varden, perhaps. Or yourself."

"Not I," Broom said, and smiled. He waved his gun. "Sit down. We're not going anywhere for the moment."

"Not to the police?"

"Not yet. I want some answers, first."

Sam said: "I made some phone calls about you, Broom. You didn't strike me as either the tourist type or as an insurance man. No one in Hartford ever heard of you. You're not in insurance."

"I'm not."

"Who are you, then?"

"Don't you think," Broom said quietly, "that I'm in a better position to ask questions? Or maybe you don't realize the position you're in. You're in a spot, Cameron. You've killed your brother. You were in love with his wife—I've checked up on you, you see—and you sailed into Maquid Cove yesterday and mixed things up with him. Ferne saw you in town today with Nora. It was obvious to her that you're still in love with the woman. I can't say I blame you much—she's damn attractive—but murdering your brother over her is going just a little too far."

"More than that," Sam said. "It's ridiculous."

"Is it? The jury would eat up a story like that."

"But you know it isn't true!"

"What I know, and what I could tell a jury, may or may not be two different things. I want you to be level with me, Cameron. Maybe you didn't kill Lyman. But someone did, and I think you know who it was."

"I wouldn't be standing here if I did."

"My gun persuades you, don't forget." Broom's teeth shone white when he smiled. Sam looked down the edge of wharf pilings toward Ferne's boat. There was no sign of activity there. He hoped she wouldn't show up here. He

felt sick, and he wanted to wipe the smile off Broom's
thin, pleased face. He remained silent. Talking would do
no good. Wait him out, he decided. And then Broom said
casually: "What did Lyman do with the money?"

"What money?" Sam asked.

"You know what I'm talking about."

He's after it, too, Sam thought. They were all after it.
Obviously, Broom and Varden were not partners, but it
was equally obvious that Varden had discounted Broom
as being inconsequential. Now Broom was after the money, and he knew Lyman had come ashore with it. What
was more important, however, was that Broom didn't
know where the money was. He hadn't seen Sam bring it
aboard. And if he had consulted Ferne, then Ferne hadn't
seen him, either. Or if she did, then she was keeping quiet
for reasons of her own.

He felt as if his thoughts were going in circles, and he
brought himself back sharply to the problem of the gun in
Broom's hand. For a moment he debated trying to jump
him, but Broom looked too competent, too much at ease
to risk such a foolhardy maneuver. He sat still, not wanting to antagonize the man any more than he had to.

Broom spoke after a little silence. "I'll tell you,
Cameron. Maybe you didn't kill Lyman. Maybe you really don't know the score. I'm not sure of you, and I like to
be sure of everybody concerned. I want to know where
they all stand. That way, I can figure my own moves
better. It's like a game of chess. Right now, I guess we've
got a stalemate."

"You've got the gun," Sam pointed out.

"But I don't have the money."

"I can't help you there."

"Maybe not . . . What do you know about Varden?"

"Practically nothing," Sam said.

"You don't know what he does for a living, who he is?"

"No."

"Yet you come to visit him."

"I came to see Lyman on business. I heard he was
staying at Maquid as Varden's guest. Varden was just a
name to me that didn't mean anything. It still doesn't mean

anything. Does the money you mentioned belong to him?"

"Perhaps. Varden is a rich man, aside from anything else. He'd have to be, owning a schooner like the Panther and Maquid Point and the house he built there. You've seen that house?"

Sam nodded. "I've seen it."

"Lots of money. Varden was in the steel business before he retired. He was in steel for only a couple of years, but they were good years for an operator like him. After the war. The newspapers called it a gray market, and I guess you could label Varden a middleman, buying and selling steel as a commodity, and acting as agent in locating it when it was in such short supply."

"I remember reading a stink in the papers about it."

"But you didn't read anything about Varden. He's one of the boys who didn't get caught."

"What's all this got to do with Lyman's murder?"

"Nothing, maybe. I'm just filling you in, because you and I are going to do some work together, tonight."

Sam said: "Go ahead. I'm listening."

"Listen hard," Broom said, and his soft, quiet voice was suddenly harsh. "You're in a spot. You're going to do as I say, but I don't want to have to watch you every second of the time. You're going to sail this boat back to Maquid, and then you and I will sit there and wait for Varden to come back there."

"What makes you think he'll go back tonight?"

Broom said: "He will. His plans depend on it."

Sam nodded toward the cabin door. "And what about Lyman?"

"We'll take him with us."

"And Ferne? Isn't she waiting to take you back?"

"She'll have to be disappointed again."

There was nothing he could do. The gun gave him no choice. Sam stood up carefully and went to work on the tangled sails.

Chapter Eleven

THE DARKNESS MADE A SOLID WALL AHEAD of them. Sam let the sloop ghost forward under jib alone, straining to make out the dark bulk of Maquid Point. There was a smell of rain in the air, and the sea had an uneasy chop that slapped hard against the Holiday's bow.

"We'll need a light," he said.

"Use your bull's-eye lantern," Eli Broom suggested.

"I can't handle the tiller and stand forward at the same time."

It was like talking into a void. He couldn't see Broom. There was nothing to see except the white loom of the jib arching beyond the mast. The run out from Haddamsport had been easy enough, following the channel buoys and shore lights; but it had taken all his skill to ease the sloop along the desolate coast to Maquid Cove. He could hear the dull boom and hiss of breakers nearby, but the direction of the sound was confusing, coming from all sides. The breeze, though light, was steady, and the Holiday made easy progress toward the anchorage. At least, Sam thought wryly, he hoped it was the anchorage.

He turned as movement sounded in the cockpit and Broom appeared beside him at the tiller. A glint of white metal revealed the lantern in his left hand.

"Do we have to use this thing?"

"Either that, or run aground," Sam said.

"All right. I'll go forward. No funny stuff, though."

Sam didn't reply. At the moment, the boat's safety was more important than a chance to tackle the man and get the gun away from him. Even that would buy him nothing. He wanted information more than Broom had told him so far, and perhaps by stringing along with Broom, he might learn a lot of answers tonight.

86

The sharp beam of light was like a soundless explosion, bursting into the darkness ahead. Dark rock loomed to port, towering over the Holiday's mast. He swung the tiller hard, heard the jib flap, and listened apprehensively for the grate of the keel on bottom. The Holiday nosed to starboard and he heard Eli Broom's whistling intake of breath. The looming bluff passed slowly alongside and then the lantern beam was lost in vague blackness that yawned ahead of them. Sam took one hand from the tiller and dried his palm on his thighs. It had been close. The anchorage opened dead ahead.

In the backlight of the lantern, Sam saw Eli Broom crouching on the bow. The beam touched the black hull of the Panther, then swung wide across the water to the pier and sail loft. The runabout was gone, and so were the dinghies. The place looked deserted. Broom played the light on the wall of underbrush beyond the beach, but no one appeared. The straw-haired man made a sound of satisfaction and looked back at Sam.

"We're here first."

"Does that mean anything?"

"Maybe. Tie up at the pier."

"What makes you so sure Varden will return?"

Broom gestured toward the Panther as they slid by. "Cas Varden won't leave the neighborhood except in the schooner. He needs the boat, and he needs someone to sail it, too. Lyman was sailing her for him, but if Varden knows Lyman is dead, he'll need another skipper. My guess is that you'll be elected."

"Why me? He could pick up a captain in Haddamsport without much trouble. For that matter, what's the matter with Nate?"

"All liquor and no brains. . . . He wouldn't want to drag a stranger into this. You're already in it, so you'd do fine."

"You seem to know a lot about Varden's plans."

Broom chuckled. "I do."

"Do they include Nora? And you?"

"Let's be patient, shall we? Let's wait and see."

At the pier, the slim man jumped ashore and made the

lines fast, then waited while Sam hauled down the jib and stowed it away. The moment it was done, he snapped out the lantern and the darkness returned, thicker than before. Broom's gun prodded Sam gently in the back.

"Let's get comfortable in the bushes back there. We might have a long wait. It depends on how soon Varden gets discouraged."

THE MOSQUITOES SANG. OFF IN THE DISTANCE, the surf boomed. There was an eternal whispering in the brush around them, a movement of the breeze and of unseen night things. Below where Sam sat, the beach and pier were a vague white patch in the darkness of the cove. When he looked at the luminous hands of his watch, he was surprised to see it was only a little after ten. He thought of Lyman, dead in his bunk aboard the sloop, the knife still in his heart, and he pondered the murderer's identity, trying to call up an image of the deed and the killer. It could be anybody. He could visualize Lyman's handsome face well enough, broken by fear, by despair and sudden terror. Or had he been taken unaware, assuming himself safe with the killer?

He felt Eli Broom tap his shoulder.

"You could have gotten away from me in this dark."

"I know that," Sam said. "Half a dozen times."

"Why didn't you?"

"I want to see what comes off here."

Broom said thoughtfully, "You're a strange fellow, Sam."

"Not so strange. I don't know what you're after—maybe it's just the money—but all I want is the knife artist who killed Lyman."

"Maybe you'll get him. Maybe you will, at that."

He heard the rustle of underbrush as Broom moved away again. The mosquitoes went on singing. The surf muttered away.

They waited.

It was after eleven before the first sound of a motor reached them. It was coming slowly, moving in out of the

vast, opaque darkness that shrouded the sea. He sat up
straighter and then heard the cold snick of the safety catch
as Broom readied his gun. Sam turned toward the man's
dim face.

"Are you planning to use that from here?"

"I like to be ready, that's all. Which boat is it?"

"I can't tell yet."

He supposed it was the runabout. It had to be, because
he would have recognized the uneasy wheeze of Ferne's
lobster boat. This was a deep-throated, powerful throb,
and he turned to watch the entrance of the anchorage. No
running lights showed, yet the volume of sound suddenly
increased, aided by the echo of the rocky bluffs that
sheltered the place.

"Is it Varden?" Broom asked.

"I think so. What do you propose to do now?"

"We'll follow him. He'll take us where we want to go."

"He'll see the Holiday. He'll know we're here."

"He'll know *you're* here," Broom said. "Not me."

"Suppose he goes aboard and finds Lyman?"

"Maybe he already knows all about Lyman."

The runabout nosed in to the pier, a dim amorphous
shadow on the surface of the water. He wondered if Nora
were aboard with Varden. He hoped not. Yet they had
been together the last time he saw them. He frowned,
thinking about this, and then another sound touched his
consciousness. A second motor came out from beyond the
cove, and he recognized it instantly as Ferne's. The people
in the runabout heard it, too, and their engine was
silenced. For just a moment afterward, the Emma G.'s
rattletrap engine wheezed and popped out there in the
darkness, and then it, too, was cut off.

"Hell," Broom muttered.

"There's two of them," Sam whispered.

"Ferne?"

"I think so. What would she be doing here?"

Broom chuckled. "Looking for you, I suppose. She's
kind of soft on you, you know."

"Don't be a fool," Sam said sharply.

Now the darkness was no longer on their side, helping

them. Sam was sure that Ferne had guided her boat into the cove, using her way to coast through the entrance in silence. Apparently she had shadowed the runabout all the way from Haddamsport, and it suddenly occurred to him that she may have done so under orders from Eli Broom. He frowned, then bent all his senses on identifying the sounds and dim movements down there on the beach.

The runabout had come in alongside the Holiday, judging from the faint bumping down there. That would be Varden, then. There followed the unmistakable scuff of shoe leather on concrete, and some of the breath eased out of his taut lungs. They hadn't spent any time aboard the Holiday. There were two of them, and they were talking, but only formless whispers reached to the underbrush where he waited. There was no trace of the Emma G. now. She hadn't come in to the landing. He reached into his memory for a chart of the cove, trying to recall how it had appeared in daylight. There was a small stretch of sandy beach just on the inward edge of the rock bluff that formed the northern arm of the anchorage. He listened, trying to pick out the sound of a keel on that sand, but nothing came to him. Still, that was where she must have touched shore.

Suddenly Nora's voice, surprisingly clear, called through the darkness.

"Sam!"

Broom's hand tightened in warning over his arm.

"Sam, are you here?" Nora called again.

Silence lapped through the dark of the night. Varden's voice came impatiently: "He must have gone to the house. Come on."

"What about the other boat?"

"Imagination. If not, it's gone by, that's all. Hurry."

Eli Broom stood up, silently, smoothly. Sam straightened with him. Footsteps sounded on the gravel path below them, nearing their hiding place. Broom didn't move until they had gone by, although the footsteps were still audible.

"Let's go," Broom whispered.

Sam took a step with him, then abruptly ducked to one

side. The dark underbrush swallowed him. He walked rapidly, heedless of the sounds he made, for another dozen paces, and then he stood stock still, not moving again. Behind him, he heard Broom's muffled curse. The other man was exasperated. He didn't dare shout or call out. Escape from him proved to be a simple matter of melting away in the darkness.

For several moments Sam waited, listening. He heard Eli Broom's footsteps hesitate and then come back toward the beach. They paused again, and then the man moved in his original direction, up the path after Varden and Nora.

Sam waited. A mosquito sang hungrily about his head, but he did not slap at it. Eventually it settled on his forearm. He let it alone. He was rewarded, presently, by the sound of other footsteps, and this time they came again from the beach. Nora and Varden were already gone. So was Broom. This would be Ferne, then. He wondered briefly where Nate was, and what he was doing, and then he returned to the path and followed after Ferne.

The way led along the pine-covered ridge. The path was just a pale glimmering of white, threading the darkness. He timed his footsteps to those of the girl's, pausing when she halted, and waiting until she went on before he, too, continued. For several minutes he followed in this manner. Varden and Nora, with Broom after them, were far out of earshot when the path swung from the woods to the beach again. Ahead, the half-timbered English house bulked dark and shapeless against the gleam of Maquid Cove. It was here that Ferne left the path and cut across the dunes. Trailing her became rapidly more difficult, almost impossible. He could only guess at her destination and her route, which consisted of a wide circle of the house and then on up the beach until they were well beyond its lights. Sam let the distance increase between Ferne and himself. He didn't think she knew he was following. Certainly, she wasn't interested in Varden's movements, or Eli Broom's.

Across the dunes, he saw the ramshackle, burned-out hotel he had studied earlier that day. Darkness hid its scorched walls, and except for an occasional stark timber, it looked surprisingly solid against the night sky. Ferne's dim figure moved purposefully across the beach and then disappeared in the deep shadows near the wall. A moment later he cut across the dunes after her and stood where she had disappeared.

There was an open doorway here, and no sign of the girl. He listened, and thought he heard the faint creak of a board from inside. He stepped across the threshold.

The darkness was absolute, and Ferne had a definite advantage now. She knew her way about the ruins. He could hear her distinctly, somewhere in the labyrinth ahead. The smell of charred wood filled the air. He sensed moderate spaciousness around him, and guessed he was in a fairly large room, perhaps the old kitchen. But for all he knew, the floor might be treacherously rotten, or full of holes that would plummet him down to the cellar. No point in breaking his neck uselessly. Yet the girl was moving farther away with each moment.

Then the darkness ahead filled with a dim radiance, outlining the room and the doorway ahead. Evidently Ferne thought it safe to use a flashlight. He moved silently forward. The light flickered and grew dim at the end of a long, musty hallway.

The corridor opened into a vast space that must have been the ballroom of the ancient hotel. He stepped on something that crunched under his weight; he didn't stop. There were rustlings all around him, and dimly outlined by the light ahead was a broad flight of rickety stairs. It was the lobby, then. He saw now the dust-shrouded clerk's desk and the sand-blown doorways facing the sea. Where the huge plate-glass windows had been were now just vast gaps in the wall.

Ferne's light flickered at the head of the stairs. He followed swiftly. There was no hesitation about the girl's path. Once she paused, as if to listen, and he stood silent in the shadows behind her. After a moment she went on.

She turned a corner, opened a door—and screamed. It was a quick, muffled sound, but even as Sam threw aside caution and plunged down the corridor toward her, he heard her fall. The beam of her flashlight shot through the

↵pen door, full on his face. For a moment he was blinded. He stood waiting, waiting for death.

Nothing happened. There was no further sound.

He moved into the room, angling out of range of the light on the floor. He saw now that Ferne had dropped it when she fell. Her body looked limp and lifeless on the floor. For a moment he felt a cold, tight knot inside him, as if a serpent coiled in his stomach. She was dead. Then he saw that she wasn't dead, she still breathed. She had simply fainted.

He reached down and picked up the flashlight and played it around the moldy, crumbling room.

"All right," he said aloud. "Come out of it."

No one answered. There was a sagging cot that had been beyond salvage when the hotel burned, and no other furniture in the room. But there was a man on the cot, and Sam stared.

It was his old man of the sea. Nora's pal—Amos Butterick.

Chapter Twelve

HE WAS DEAD. HIS HEAD HUNG DOWN OVER THE thin mattress, and his bulging blue eyes stared in blind horror at the bright beam of the flashlight. He still wore the same filthy clothing Sam had seen before. He played the light over the fragile, broken body, picking out the mutilated hands, the tattered, bloody feet. The blood looked old and dark and crusted on the clothing.

The thought came to him that this was the man who first created Nora Jordan, a woman to fit the image of his dreams. Perhaps he had possessed her, too. It seemed as if Amos Butterick, and New York, were long, long lost in the past.

In a way, the old man must have been happy to die, in

view of his tortures. Someone had vented a vicious sadism
upon him, before he somehow found a way to the dory
and escaped Maquid Point, only to be returned by the
Holiday. But why the torture? He thought of the money
Lyman had tried to escape with, and some of it made
sense, but not all of it.

He looked at Ferne. Her face was upturned to the light
like some dim, night-blooming flower, her dark hair in a
lustrous wealth about her head. Had she expected to find
the old man here? She had known where she was going. It
had to be the old man.

He frowned, puzzling over it. Under the window-sill,
scattered on the floor, were two crumpled paper bags, an
open can that had contained chicken soup, and an empty
vacuum jug. He picked up the jug. The dregs of coffee
were in the bottom. Maybe Ferne had brought food here
for the old man. Still frowning, Sam paused and listened.
The huge old building was full of creaks and groans and
whisperings that came from everywhere and nowhere.

Ferne was surprisingly light when he gathered her up in
his arms. Light and warm and soft to the touch. Sam
reflected with a shock that he had never really thought of
her as a mature woman, and he had never been more
mistaken. He stowed the flashlight in his pocket, deciding
its light was too dangerous to use now, and felt sharp
relief when he finally reached the sandy lobby floor and
stepped through the yawning front doors to the beach.

The cool night air made Ferne stir in his arms. He
walked with her to the dunes, feeling curiously excited,
and put her down gently. The breeze rustled in the coarse
grass, and the gentle surf added to the sounds of the night.
He sat still and watched her as she suddenly opened her
eyes and struggled to sit up.

"Don't scream again," he said quietly.

Her eyes were enormous, trying to identify him in the
dark.

"Sam?"

He felt pleased. "It's all right. You just fainted."

She looked sharply behind her at the dark hulk of the

el, then at him again. "How did you know I was in there?"

"I followed you. I was waiting at the cove when you landed."

"But Nora called to you. Didn't you hear?"

"I heard," he said. "I waited for you."

She was silent a moment. "Is that supposed to mean something?"

"Now don't pick a quarrel again," he said. "Take that chip off your shoulder for a minute, can't you? I won't bite. If you were in any danger from me, you wouldn't have wakened out here."

"I'm not afraid of you," Ferne said.

"That's fine. What *are* you afraid of, then? What made you yip and faint up there?"

"I—I didn't expect to find the old man dead, I guess." Her face was too dim in the shadows for him to be sure of her expression. She sat there, hugging her knees, and stared out at the dark ocean. "I still don't know who he was. Do you?"

"I think his name is Amos Butterick. Mean anything?"

Her laugh was bitter. "My stepfather worked for him."

"Varden?"

"They were partners, sort of. But I never met Butterick before. He was just a name, that's all."

"You should have told me about hiding him up here. He was in a coma when I left him; you couldn't have carried him to the hotel yourself. Who helped you?"

"Eli Broom," Ferne said. "He was with me. The old man wasn't in a coma then. He was delirious, though. He crawled out of your boat and was on hands and knees on the path, trying to follow you. Eli and I found him there. Eli suggested hiding him in the hotel."

"Why?"

"He didn't say."

"He must have given you some reason. Why didn't he suggest taking him to the south shore, to your house?"

"He didn't want me involved. And he thought Nate might learn about him."

"Then why didn't he take him to the doc, in Haddai. port?"

"Eli said he was dying. He said it was just a matter of hours. The old man had been tortured so inhumanly. . . ."

Sam nodded. "I still don't know why Broom hid him here."

"He was hoping Butterick might say what had happened to him. But he didn't. He passed out, and we both sat there in that horrible building, trying to make him comfortable; but he didn't know where he was, and raved about all sorts of things, and finally he fell asleep. He was asleep, he wasn't dead, when we left him. I wanted to take him to Dr. McReadie, but Eli said it was no use; if we tried to move him that far, the old man would die."

"What did Broom expect to learn from him?" Sam asked.

"I don't know."

"Where does Broom fit into all this, anyway?"

Ferne was silent.

Sam said irritably: "You still don't trust me?"

"It was you who brought the old man back here, when he was trying to escape from Maquid."

"I didn't know anything about it when I picked him up."

"That's what Eli said. He said the old man had been kept a prisoner here, and that you and your friends wanted something from him, and that's why he was tortured."

"And Broom included me in the deal?"

"That's what he said."

"Do you believe everything he says?"

Ferne was silent, hugging her knees, staring at the sea. He remembered how she had felt in his arms, and he didn't move, waiting for her to make up her mind. Suddenly it was important that she trust him. He was in hot water, plenty of it. But it was more than just having someone believe that his visit to Maquid had been innocent. Whatever his motives, they hadn't included murder. He wanted Ferne to believe that, Ferne especially.

"Look," he said. "You and Broom saw me bring in the

old man. You saw me leave him. So Broom waited and watched the old fellow crawl after me and then you picked him up and took him here. Later you found me loopy in your boat, not knowing what I was doing. You hauled me home and put me to bed. How can you figure I was involved, when I was obviously just another victim?"

She was silent. Then she said: "This used to be a lovely place. Now everything is wrong with it. I don't know what's happened since Varden came here. It's not the same. I used to think I'd fight tooth and nail to keep the Point for myself, but I'd just as soon let him have it, now."

"What claim does Varden have to it?"

"He says he can break my mother's will. She owned all of Maquid. She left most of it to me when she died."

"What about Nate? Was he here when I landed, or at your house?"

"I don't know where he was. The first I saw of him was this morning. You were there." Ferne stood up suddenly. "Come on. I don't want to stay here all night. I want to go home."

"What do we do about the old man?"

"Let Eli Broom decide about that."

Sam said: "This Broom certainly leads you around by the hand. Do you let him decide about everything?"

"Why not? He knows more about it than I do."

"How do you know he's not working with Varden?"

"He isn't," Ferne said simply.

"But how do you know?" he insisted.

Ferne took a deep breath. "I guess you'll find out from him, now that Butterick is dead. He'll have to do something about it. And he will, you see. Because he's a detective."

Chapter Thirteen

SAM STOOD UP WITH HER. FERNE LOOKED anxious. He bent down and picked up her flashlight, but he didn't thumb the button. In the gloom, his face was impassive, except for the quick knot of muscle along the ridge of his jaw. Finally he said:

"How long have you known that Broom was a cop?"

"From the beginning. When he first came, posing as an insurance man, I noticed he was more interested in the Panther and Varden than in surf casting. He didn't know the first thing about bass, even if he pretended to. He just didn't act like the person he said he was, that's all."

"How long has he been here?"

"Yesterday was two weeks." She started walking slowly across the dunes, as if to cut across the high ridge of the Point and return home that way. Sam moved to keep up with her, his arm brushing hers as they walked along in the dark. He was pleased that the antagonism was gone from her voice when she said: "I learned Broom was a detective by accident. He didn't want me to know. But his wallet gave him away, of course."

"How did you get to his wallet?"

"He went swimming one night—and he couldn't find where he'd left his pants." He heard Ferne's soft laugh. "It was funny at the time. Anyway, I went down to the beach next morning and found his clothes. His wallet had spilled out of the back pocket and was spilled open, and there was a badge pinned in it, so I knew he was a detective."

"What else?" Sam asked.

"I didn't look any further. But as soon as Nate left, I asked Eli about it. He admitted it, and said he was staying nere because he had a job to do. And then he asked me to help, if I could, and I said I would of course."

"Does Nate know Broom is a detective?"

"I don't think so."

"Did Broom say if he was a local or federal man?"

Ferne was thoughtful. "I gathered he was checking on Varden for income-tax purposes, and that would make him federal."

"Maybe. Or else he's just looking to make a pretty piece of change for himself."

His voice was savage. Ferne stared. "What do you mean?"

"I think he took you. Maybe Broom really is a cop, but he could be working on his own. He doesn't operate the way a cop should. There's been a murder committed, but he isn't in any great rush to do anything about it. There's money in this thing, and he might be trying to get some to line that wallet of his."

"You sound pretty sure of it."

"I'm sure of one thing," he said. "No ordinary cop would be as complacent about murder as Eli Broom seems to be."

He was thinking of Lyman, dead aboard his sloop, but Ferne didn't know about Lyman yet. Her footsteps faltered, and he took her arm, then let his fingers find hers. She didn't take her hand from his. Her whole body shuddered slightly.

"Who do you think did it?" she asked, whispering. "Who could have tortured the old man like that?"

"I'm pretty sure Amos Butterick came to Maquid aboard the Panther, with the others. Broom knew they were coming and waited to see what he could see. I can guess why they tortured him, and I wouldn't be too far wrong. It's not important right now. What is more important is that you get off the Point and stay somewhere that might be safe."

"Don't frighten me," Ferne said. "Nobody would bother me."

He said earnestly: "You admit only you and Broom knew where Butterick was hidden after I brought him ashore. Look, Ferne. Whatever they wanted from him, they haven't got yet, regardless of the tortures they applied to Butterick. The old man disappeared, and I brought him back, innocently enough. As soon as I landed, I was slugged to give them a chance to question him again. But they couldn't find him, because you and Broom hid him in the hotel. Now he's dead, and his secret is dead with him. But they'll think you know, you and Broom, and they'll come for you next, to make you talk."

"But he didn't tell me anything!" Ferne protested.

"They won't believe you. Anyway, you still know too much to be safe. They can't let you run around loose and talk about it in Haddamsport, for instance."

Ferne paused. They had come to the top of the ridge, by a path she had picked out of the dark. The ruined monastery bulked ahead. Beyond, the land fell away through unburned pine woods toward Ferne's house. The path led across a leveled area surrounded by a high, vine-grown stone wall that had once enclosed a garden. Again Sam was touched by the indescribable loneliness of the place. The tumbled walls, the deep cellar pits, the lone Gothic arch that survived centuries of neglect. Ferne started forward again, picking her way with care until they came to an irregular cloister composed of a small series of arches. Underfoot, the flagstones had heaved and were overgrown. Still holding Sam's hand, Ferne drew him forward until he made out a stone bench that stood against the mass of a shattered flying buttress.

"You know your way around here pretty well," he said.

"I've played up here since I was a child."

"And never afraid of ghosts?"

"Sometimes," she said. Again the quick shudder ran through her as they sat down. "I had enough imagination, as a child. In the daylight was best, because then I could dream safely. Then the sun was shining and there was blue sea all around and there couldn't be anything to fear. I used to think of the French monks who built this place, and then I'd imagine how it was when the Indians came and burned down the first church here. Later, I imagined pirates and smugglers. There's supposed to be buried trea-

..re on Maquid, you know. And once in a while I'd come here at night, when there was a moon."

"Alone?" Sam asked.

"Not always. There were boys from Haddamsport."

"But none now?"

"No. None."

"Why not?"

"I don't know. Maybe because of Nate. He's been pretty horrible lately."

"He's due for a reckoning," Sam said.

They were silent, sitting together in the darkness that clung to the wall. He felt strangely isolated, as if the ruins no longer belonged to sea, wind or stars. Nothing really existed here. He tried to imagine Ferne coming here as a child to play. He preferred not to think of her coming here in later years with young men from Haddamsport, and he was surprised at his jealousy as he pushed the thought from his mind. For the moment he was content to pause, sorting out the conflicting ideas that came forward, each claiming a solution to his predicament. He saw a pattern in it somewhere, and he saw its vague outline, but predominating all else was the danger to Ferne. She was in deadly danger. The danger touched him, too. But he had no intention of running from it.

She was sobbing quietly for several moments before he realized it, and then the shock of it left him discomfited. He wanted to put his arms around her, but he didn't know what her reaction to that would be.

"Ferne," he said.

"I—I'm sorry."

"Ferne, what is it?"

He spoke quietly, earnestly: "Ferne, I told you I'm on your side. I won't let anything happen to you."

"I'm afraid, all right. But it's not that."

"Then what is it?"

"Nothing," she said again. "It doesn't matter." She scrubbed her cheeks with the palms of her hands. "It's been a long time since I cried. Since I sat up here with anyone."

"Who was he?" Sam asked.

"A boy. He went into the Navy when the war bega_ He liked it here, too. He liked the sea. He had a lot of ideas about re-designing the fishing draggers used around here, and they were good ideas, too. You'd have liked him. He never came back, of course. He was killed in the Pacific. So I stopped coming up here."

"Is that why you were crying?"

"That's partly it." In the pale starlight her face was like a night flower. "I've been sick ever since," she whispered. "Sick inside, I mean. Like you're sick, too."

"I?"

"The way you feel about Nora."

"I don't——"

"You lost her, and I lost Alex. I never thought I'd talk this way to another man again. Maybe it's the way you remind me of Alex. Your boat, the way you look at the sea. I—I have a foolish idea. I think we could cure each other of our sickness."

He couldn't breath. "Ferne. . . ."

She turned on the bench to face him. "Sam?"

He wondered. He knew she was shivering, and knew it wasn't from the cool sea wind. Hunger grew in him, shaking him. He couldn't attempt to explain what had happened to him. Hour by hour she had grown inside him. Her eyes, large and luminous, looked anguished. Her voice was smothered.

"Sam . . ."

It was like an explosion between them, this thing that happened. She was in his arms. He could feel the vibrant pliancy of her form, and his lips searched her eyes, touched the dark wealth of her hair, found her responsive mouth. He wanted her, and she wanted him, and he knew she was right, and what they were doing was right, that it was good and right. The stars reeled drunkenly in the night sky, and the sea shimmered and shone, and the broken Gothic arches leaned over them like a benediction. Her body was like an unguent, enfolding him, soothing and healing him.

For long moments afterward, they were silent. There

was only the wind in the pines and the distant mutter of the sea. The stars returned to their appointed places.

"Ferne?"

"It's all right."

She combed her hair, and Sam watched the shimmering, tumbled glory of it. Something had happened inside him, something more than was indicated simply by that which was between them now. Her face was impassive, neither smiling nor unfriendly. He knew she didn't want to talk about it for the moment, and he understood, if the chaos inside her was anything like what he felt himself.

He looked at his watch.

"We'd better move on. We can make it back to the anchorage now, I guess. You'd better take the Emma G. and head straight for Haddamsport. Don't go home to pack anything."

She looked at him. "Are you going to stay here?"

"I've some business to finish. Not what you think, Ferne. I've told you the truth about myself; I wasn't mixed up in this until tonight, but now I'm in too deep to back out. I have to settle this for myself."

"But it's as dangerous for you as it is for me."

"It will be easier if I know you're safe," Sam said. "In Haddamsport, I'd suggest you stay with some friends or in a tourist home. Some place where Nate or Varden can't find you. I'll get in touch with you as soon as I can."

"I can stay with Alex's father—Dr. McReadie."

Sam understood that Alex was the boy who had enlisted in the Navy. He was glad that she could mention him easily now.

"All right. Let's get going."

They moved out from under the arches to the uneven stones of a terrace. To one side, a hole gaped in the ground, overgrown with weeds in what had once been a vaulted cellar. He saw now that the path Ferne had followed was well defined, although it was lost at the moment in the ruined foundations all around them.

He wasn't quite sure when he first heard the muted padding of paws, the sharp click of a claw on stone. Ferne heard it, too.

"It's the dog," she whispered. "Varden's dog."

"Would he be alone?"

She shook her head. "I hardly think so."

Sam stooped and found a stone on the ground tha[t] fitted the palm of his hand. For a long moment they wer[e] motionless, not breathing, with the dog's paws clickin[g] closer behind them. He heard the heavy snuffing of the bi[g] animal and visualized the powerful jaws and the viciou[s] temperament, trained for destruction. A moment later h[e] heard the soft scrape of a man's footsteps behind the dog[.] Someone was looking for them here. Fortunately, th[e] breeze was downwind from the dog to them, and h[e] hadn't gotten their scent yet.

A low wall paralleled the path where they waited, an[d] he realized the man and the dog were on the other side[,] coming in the same direction. The wall ended in tumble[d] stones and then the brush began again, sloping down int[o] the woods to the water. In a moment the dog would reac[h] the end of the wall and meet them face to face.

He touched Ferne's shoulder in warning.

"Start running," he whispered. "I'll stop the dog."

"But I——"

"I'll see you in Haddamsport."

Turning, he walked ahead without attempt at conceal[-] ment. On the opposite side of the wall, the dog barke[d] explosively. Sam didn't have time to see what Ferne wa[s] doing. The Dobie was a long dark shape, spinning aroun[d] the rubble, moving with ferocious speed. Footsteps clat[-] tered to the rear. He just had time to fling up an arm t[o] ward off the dog as it launched itself. The impact knocke[d] him backward, and he thought he heard someone scream[.] The wall saved him. The dog's teeth grazed his arm, an[d] it thudded hard against the mossy stones. It whirled, fur[y] in its throat as it gathered to spring again. Sam swun[g] hard with the stone in his hand. The dog dropped with [a] flat thud. At the same moment, the night exploded wit[h] light as the man who followed turned a flash on him.

"Drop the rock!"

Sam let the stone fall. The dog was only stunned, it[s] flanks heaving; the steel linked collar around its nec[k] glittered in the light, as if it were bejeweled. In the moment's pause, he listened to learn if Ferne had escaped, but there was no sound except the tread of the man's footsteps behind him.

"Turn around."

The flashlight blinded him, then swung away in a swift circle of the ruins. Ferne was gone. He drew a breath of relief that was abruptly halted as he saw the long, double-barreled shotgun in the other's hand. A familiar shotgun. He had seen it before, and felt it, too, on the Holiday earlier that day.

"Take it easy, Nate," he said.

The man was like a behemoth in the backwash of light. He wore a sweatshirt and dungarees, stuffed into cowhide boots. He swung a short leather leash from his left hand, and grinned.

"Good thing you didn't kill the mutt."

"The Dobie will be all right," Sam said. "Not that he did me any good."

"He'd kill you," Nate said. "Where is Ferne?"

"She wasn't with me."

"Matey, I ain't stupid. When we couldn't find you, I figured you both came here. We got everybody but you and Ferne now."

"Everybody?"

"Eli Broom, too. Mr. Varden's got some questions for you." The fat man snapped the leash on the dog's collar. The Doberman was showing signs of life again. "I ain't worried about Ferne. She won't get far. I got every boat here gimmicked. Unless they swim or try the beaches, nobody leaves Maquid Point without our say-so."

Chapter Fourteen

THERE WAS NO WAY TO GET PAST THE DOG. IT sat there, hating him, red tongue lolling, half crouched on its haunches at the far end of the taut leash. Its quick, urgent breathing panted back and forth from the damp stone walls around him.

He was alone, except for the dog. He had been alone for some time, his hands and feet securely lashed. Nate had tied the knots with grim relish, drawing them so tight that the first warning tingles of closed circulation were already gone from his arms and legs, replaced by the numbness that worried him. No use trying to loosen the knots himself; he had tried that, and his efforts only tightened them. He could only hope that someone would return soon. Nobody could have heard him if he called for help.

It was a fix, he thought, yet he wanted it, knowing that Lyman's death couldn't be solved otherwise. Even before he made Ferne escape, he knew he was going to let Varden find him. He hoped she would elude Nate, that was all. He tried to catch the sound of the Emma G.'s motor, but the quick, frantic breathing of the Dobie covered everything.

The dog tried to hitch nearer him, and the knot at the end of the leash seemed to slip a bit. He lay still, watching the dog's baleful eyes. The moon had come out, and it shone behind fragmentary clouds, making his surroundings more unreal than before.

He was in an old wine cellar of the monastery, somewhere in the honeycomb of ancient foundations and subterranean corridors. The cellars were better preserved than the rest of the structure, and this particular room had been occupied not too long since.

Only part of the floor above remained, supported on rudimentary columns. The gaping hole above admitted enough moonlight to give him a picture of the place. There was a cot shoved against the stone wall in one corner, and a rickety wooden table on which stood several empty bottles and a guttered stub of candle. The dog sat in front of the only entrance. He wondered if this was where the old man, Butterick, had been imprisoned and tortured, and if it were, how he had managed to escape. Perhaps through the jagged hole in the ceiling. If he could get up on the table, it might be done. If he weren't tied, hand and foot. And if he wanted to, at the moment, which he didn't.

He lay still and waited, watching the dog.

The numbness had gone through both arms and legs before he heard footsteps on the stones overhead. A flashlight danced on the moss-grown walls. The dog's ears twitched, but he didn't move his baleful yellow gaze from Sam. Someone said: "Satan is still here. It's all right. I'll get after the girl again."

That was Nate's grumbling voice. Varden's reply was impatient. "Never mind Ferne. You couldn't find her anywhere tonight. She could be hiding in a thousand places."

The light disappeared, and then the crude curtain was thrust aside and Varden stepped into the cellar. The man's attitude expressed extreme distaste for his surroundings. He murmured to the dog and glanced at Sam, nodded, and took the lantern from Nate and placed it on the rickety table. Sam blinked in the sudden glare. Something squeaked and scampered swiftly out of sight into a corner.

"These rats," Varden murmured. "Good evening, Sam."

"I wish you'd loosen these knots," Sam said. "Nate was too enthusiastic when he tied them."

Varden looked annoyed and signed to the big man. Nate came forward, muttering, and freed the rope enough so that the danger from lost circulation was relieved. Nate went back then and picked up his shotgun and grinned at Sam. "Mr. Varden has some questions to ask you, mate."

Varden said: "It is not a joking matter. I would rather this had not happened. I had hoped that you and I, Mr. Cameron, could come to an amicable agreement."

"About what?"

"A number of things. Violence is wasted when it must be applied to a man like you. I dislike making enemies—particularly dangerous enemies. It is not a matter of cowardice on my part, but rather of expediency. One does not alienate men who are needed for one's plans."

"You have plans for me?" Sam asked.

"You have been included in them since your arrival on Maquid. You suit my purposes far better than your brother Lyman."

"Did you figure I'd take Lyman's place after you killed him?"

A little spasm twisted Varden's face. "I did not kill him."

"Am I expected to believe that?"

"Just now, it is immaterial what you believe. It is most essential, however, that you realize that only by cooperation can your safety, and the safety of others, be assured."

"What others?"

"Nora, for one."

Sam said: "Nora is working with you."

"She thinks she is. There is a difference." Varden paused. Nate stood across the room, his thick fingers idly scratching behind the dog's ears. Sam said nothing, waiting, and Varden sighed. "You came here to settle your business interests with Lyman, did you not? And also to see Nora. I have learned of your previous attachment to Nora, and how your brother stole her from you, so to speak. She is a beautiful woman. It would be regrettable if any violence had to be used on her, as well as on you."

"For a guy who wants everything to be beer and skittles," Sam said, "you talk a lot of violence, Casper. Just what was Lyman supposed to do that you think I can do better?"

"We will come to that later," Varden said impatiently.

"First, I must know what you learned from the old man you rescued."

"That's easy," Sam said. "Nothing."

"Nothing at all?"

"He didn't say anything to me. He couldn't. You and Nate had done too thorough a job on him."

"Then what did he tell my step-daughter, Ferne?"

Sam shrugged. "You'll have to ask her. I wouldn't know."

Nate stopped scratching the dog's ears and slouched forward. "I told you, Mr. Varden, he and Ferne were in it together, all the time. They hid the old man in the hotel. That's where they were before I caught 'em, and anything the old man told Ferne, he told this monkey, too. He told them about the money, anyway. If you'll just let me work on him a little, I'll get it out of him."

"That may not be necessary," Varden said. "I think Cameron is prepared to be reasonable. I have an idea, Nate, that he wouldn't have been caught so easily if he hadn't desired this discussion in the first place."

"How right you are," Sam said.

Varden seemed pleased. "See here, we know you and Ferne hid the old man after you rescued him at sea. Perhaps you are telling the truth when you say he gave you no information. I am inclined to believe you. After all, you were in Haddamsport before Nora and I got there, and Lyman was alone on the Point. We thought he was in a drunken stupor, and so we were not concerned with what he might do. Unfortunately, it seems now that Lyman was playing his own game. He apparently stumbled on the hideout you and Ferne prepared for the old man, and as soon as we left for Haddamsport, Lyman went to the hotel and managed to get the truth from our old fellow. Rather astonishing, in view of our past failures, but there you are. Perhaps with death so near, he divulged the information we had all been hoping to get. In any case, Lyman came to Haddamsport with the money."

"Whose money is it?" Sam asked.

Varden smiled. "Mine."

"Yours, if you get your hands on it," Sam corrected.

"I intend to accomplish that. You will tell me where it is. After that, we can discuss your part in our plans to dispose of it."

Sam said: "You're sure Lyman had the money in Haddamsport?"

"Of course."

"Then what makes you think I have it now?"

"Because Lyman is dead, aboard your sloop."

"And who killed him?"

Varden shrugged. "Perhaps you did."

"Would I be fool enough to bring the money back here, then?"

"What did you do with it?"

"I don't have it," Sam said.

"Nonsense. Lyman came to your boat and was killed there. He must have had the money with him. You have it now."

"I don't."

"I should dislike very much to turn you over to Nate. His methods are not as civilized as mine."

"I'm sorry," Sam said. "If you're planning on taking me into partnership on the basis of learning where the money is from me, you're due for a disappointment. I can't help you on that."

"I won't argue with you," Varden warned. "Is that final?"

"Yes."

Varden turned. "Nate?"

The big man came forward, grinning. "You bet, Mr. Varden."

"I leave him to you. Just don't kill him. I need him alive, no matter what he knows. You have a free hand, otherwise."

"It will be a pleasure," Nate said.

Varden unslipped the leash on the Doberman, pulling the dog back as it lunged for Sam. He looked questioningly at Sam once more, then shrugged and backed out of the cellar room, parting the canvas curtain over the entrance and then drawing it tight from the outside. Sam inched up to sit a little straighter with his back against the stone wall. His arms and legs tingled painfully as circulation returned. Nate took his time, peeling off his sweatshirt to expose his hairy torso, flexing his thick fingers and moving the table off to one side. Then he took a cigar from his dungaree pocket, straightened one mashed end, and lighted it, rolling it between his lips and regarding Sam with amusement over the flickering match flame.

"I been lookin' forward to this, mate."

Sam said: "You're a fool. So is your boss. I want a cut in this deal, not the same treatment the old man got."

"What you want and what I give you are two different things, mate. There's only one thing me and Varden wants. The money. You tell me where it is right now, and maybe we can speed things up, huh?"

Sam said: "Did you kill Lyman, Nate?"

"I'll ask the questions."

"Are you going to kill me, too, Nate?"

"Varden don't want me to, but I might, accidental like. Especially if you make me sore. Especially if you don't talk fast and tell us where you hid the money."

"I don't have it," Sam said.

Nate put his cigar down carefully on the edge of the table and slapped him, open-handed, across the mouth. Sam's head snapped back with the blow and struck the stone wall behind him. His ears rang. Numbness spread across the lower part of his face.

"You can yell all you want," Nate said. His voice was thick. "I don't mind noise. Varden is a little squeamish about stuff like this, but I don't mind it at all."

"You missed your calling," Sam muttered. "You belonged with the Nazis."

Nate chuckled. "Where is the money?"

"To hell with you," Sam said.

Nate struck him with his fist. Sam fell sidewise, helpless with his arms and ankles tied. Nate kicked him with his booted foot. He felt blood wash warm and salty through his mouth. He gagged on it, coughing, and Nate reached down and hauled him upright again. The question, the blow, and the kick were repeated. And repeated again. After that Nate reached for his smoldering cigar and said:

"Now the fun begins . . ."

PAIN JUICED THROUGH HIM IN GREAT, SHOCK-ing waves. He floated on a sea of torment, helpless to sink or swim, rising and falling in waves. Light alternated with darkness. There was the smell of charred woodland and the damp mold of the monastery cellars and the clean sting of salt water on his face. He floated on, in a mael-strom of sound, crashing and battering against raw nerves. Through the confusion some voices gabbled at him, some pitched high, others low, reaching him through the curtain of other sounds. After a time he no longer heard what the voices said. The sea of pain dissolved and then came back again. Time did not exist. The past and present whirled in a common vortex with the future.

After a time he found his bonds were gone and he was able to swim instead of float on the dark seas around him. He made walking movements, and someone supported him while he crossed the dark, burning waves. He wanted to sink, to drift slowly down into the cool darkness, but a voice kept reproaching him and he had no choice but to go endlessly forward.

Presently he was back in the vortex of time again, his memories spinning and confused. The boatyard, with its clean warm sunlight in the windows, and the smell of the sea and lumber, the distant pounding of caulk hammers on the newest hull. Later, he danced with Nora, alone in a vast nightclub draped in velvety blackness. Muted, savage music pulsed everywhere, and Nora drew him down to her, demanding, using him, smothering him until he wished for the sunlight and the brightness of the sea.

The whirlpool sucked his strength and pulled him into the cool, spinning darkness where life ended, began, and ended again. . . .

He opened his eyes to sunlight. He was confused, remembering how he had awakened another time with Ferne Dolson, remembering their hour on the hilltop, and for a while he thought it was part of his dream. Someone said, "Hello, Sam," and he thought it was Ferne; then he turned his head and saw it was Nora.

She was smiling, leaning over him, her bronze hair catching the sun. "You're all right, darling. Nate was over-enthusiastic. Casper and I stopped him. But you're fine now."

Darkness crouched in the corners of his mind.

"Sam?" Nora said.

The darkness retreated. He was aware of pain. He groaned. The pain was in his feet, his head, his face. He rolled aside and felt the pull of a cool white sheet over him.

"Sleep a while, darling," Nora said.

He slept.

It was hours later when he awoke, and the sun still shone, but Nora was gone. He felt better. The pain was greatly lessened. His face and jaws felt stiff. He was in the same bed, the same room. Through the window he could see the glimmering water of the northern sea, the desolate reach of empty coast. He sat up carefully and looked around. He was in Varden's house, an upstairs bedroom. The room was furnished impersonally, designed for guests, but it was cheerful, with bright yellow walls and white woodwork. There were two doors, one opposite the bed, the other to his right.

The second door opened while he looked at it, and Eli Broom came in from the bathroom beyond. The sandy-haired man stood in bare feet, wearing only dungarees. A strip of surgical tape was stuck to his scholarly forehead, the white sterility of the bandage in sharp contrast to his sun-reddened complexion.

"Welcome to our ivory tower, Sam," he grinned.

"So they got you, too?"

Broom nodded. "But I escaped a workout. That Nate is something. They couldn't get you to talk this way, so now they'll try to tease it out of you with kindness. Anyway, nobody's moving until they get what they want."

"The money?" Sam asked.

"Nothing but. Hungry?" Broom crossed the bedroom

on his naked feet and picked up a tray nearby. There was an electric percolator and sandwiches covered with a linen napkin. "Your girl-friend left these. Lunch in our frilly little jail. She was plenty worried about you. Made me kind of envious."

"What about Ferne?" Sam asked.

"Gone. Nate is looking, and I hope he never finds her. He has a few special ideas about her that he's been nursing."

"So that's it," Sam said. "I've wondered."

"He's made a pass or two. Not easily discouraged." Broom poured coffee for Sam. "Stoke up. You need lots of nourishment."

He was surprised at his hunger. The coffee was weak, but hot. Afterward, he collected his clothing draped over a chair. Pain shot through his feet with the first step, and he winced. Eli Broom handed him his pants with a wry smile. "That Nate."

"I'm going to kill him," Sam said.

"Save a little piece for me."

He tried standing again, and this time endured the pain. He limped to the window. He had been right about the second-story bedroom; but there was no lawn below, no ground. This wall of the house was built on the lip of rock that overhung the sea. It was a long way down. At the bottom, the surf seethed with savage strength. He gave up the idea of escape that way, and considered the door.

"What's keeping us here?"

"Look for yourself. But move fast," Broom said.

Oddly, the door was bolted on the inside. Sam pushed the barrel aside and inched it open. Instantly there came a rush of paws and the Doberman lunged against the door, almost bursting it from his grip. He glimpsed an anteroom beyond before he slammed it shut. The dog lunged again. Sam threw the bolt home and turned back.

Broom sat on the edge of the bed, smoking. "Nice pet. A war dog that wasn't rehabilitated. It wouldn't help to get into that other room, anyway. The hall-door is locked— from the outside. Far as I can see, we stay here until

Varden chooses to let us out—which means until you tell him where the money is."

"Do you think I know?" Sam asked.

Broom shrugged. "If you wouldn't tell Nate, you won't tell me. Which is too bad, because if we fight each other, Varden will win. Did Ferne tell you about me last night?"

"She said you were a cop," Sam said.

Broom laughed. "Yes. Kicked off the Boston metropolitan two years ago. A little matter of graft. I got some, but not all. Most of it went upstairs. It was the usual thing—protecting bookies and a numbers outfit. If I raised a stink about what I knew, I'd get framed, demoted, or kicked out. So I fell in line. A sour mistake. I was honest up to then, and should have stayed that way."

"How do you tie into this up here?"

"I'm free lancing. Looking for buried treasure."

"Smuggler's gold?"

"A lot of poppycock. If there ever was any buried treasure on Maquid, it was either burned up or removed by the monks, or found long ago by somebody who kept quiet in order to save taxes."

"Go on," Sam said.

"That's all I have to say. It's your turn."

"You posed as a cop to Ferne. You had a badge."

"Anybody can get a piece of tin. I've got a private license out of New York State. It doesn't mean anything here, of course. I just carried it in case I could impress anyone with it."

"Does Varden know who you are?"

"Nate hung this eye on me. I talk easily. That's my nature. But you don't like to talk at all, Sam, and I know you have a lot to talk about."

"What happens if I tell Varden where the money is?"

"You'll be all right. He can use you. Me, I get my throat cut, because they don't need me."

"How can they use me?"

"Ask Nora. She knows."

Sam was silent. He limped into the bathroom and filled the tumbler with water and drank deeply. The tiny window opened on the same wall as the bedroom windows, and there was no other doorway. He looked at himself in the mirror and winced at the welts and contusions that disfigured his face. Nora had done some amateur doctoring, but he looked as if he had single-handedly fought the Battle of Bull Run—and lost. Opening the cabinet, he found it empty except for tooth paste, two new toothbrushes, and his white gold wristwatch. He strapped the watch back on his wrist and returned to the bedroom.

From beyond the door he heard the soft, restless pacing of the Doberman. There was no other sound in the house, yet he doubted that the place was deserted. Eli Broom stretched on the bed with his hands clasped under his head and spoke amusedly.

"Save your strength, Sam. I want you to hold out. And don't let the beautiful Nora beguile you, for my sake. The minute you tell 'em where the money is, off goes my head."

"You're pretty sure I know where it is."

"Well, Lyman had it. Varden doesn't have it, neither do I. It's a process of elimination. Varden is looking for it, so am I, therefore you know where it is."

"Maybe Lyman hid it and none of us will ever find it."

"I doubt it. Lie down and relax, Sam."

"I'm worried about Ferne."

Broom leaned his weight on one elbow, his eyebrows lifted. "I thought you were crazy about Nora."

"Nora is doing all right."

Broom said: "You're learning. About the birds and the bees, I mean. Take the bees, for instance. The queen bee, especially. You know much about the queen bee, Sam?"

"You're driveling," Sam said.

"Listen and learn. Everybody thinks the queen bee is such an admirable character. Actually, she's a despot, a grabber, a spoiler. She uses the males for her own pleasure and profit, and drives the workers to kill themselves, to line her hive with honey. Her relations with other bees are selfish. All she's interested in is honey, and how to get the other bees to bring it to her." Broom paused. "Nora is a queen bee. She's a queen bee and she uses males for her own pleasure and profit, and when she's through with 'em, she doesn't care if they live or die."

"End lesson one," Sam said.

"Take it to heart," Broom grinned.

Sam stretched out on the bed. His nerves felt dulled by the pain he had endured. He should never have let Ferne try to escape alone. But maybe she was safely off the Point. But he still couldn't count on her silence. If the police moved in now, he himself would be the fall guy. Ferne didn't know about Lyman's death, but the police would learn about it, and they would follow Broom's reasoning—they'd assume he killed his brother because of the money and Nora. Only he could help himself, he decided. It was Varden's word against his. He couldn't even depend on Broom. Broom had been the first to suggest his guilt.

Sam closed his eyes and dozed.

He awoke late that afternoon. Broom sat by the window, studying the sea. Beyond the door, the dog still panted and waited. But there was a new note in the air, a mechanical vibration that made him move stiffly toward the window. A schooner moved offshore, proceeding under power. It was the Panther, sleek and black. Her progress was methodical, ranging back and forth. He guessed Nate had reassembled the engine for a test. The schooner swung hard to port and came about. The motor throbbed, and white foam boiled, while the wake spun out astern at full speed. A moment later the Panther disappeared, heading southeast around the Point.

Eli Broom moved beside him. "Think you can sail her?"

"She's sweet. Where is Nate taking her?"

"He's got a chore to do. He won't be back until evening, unless he's lucky to find a spot where there are no other boats in sight." Broom felt under his crumpled pillow and poked a finger into an empty pack of cigarettes. "The room service here is terrible. Wish I had a smoke."

"What kind of chore?" Sam asked.

Broom looked at him, his youngish face sober. "They

found Lyman's body on your sloop, you know, and they'd rather not have that kind of evidence scattered around Maquid. There's the old man's corpse, too. I gathered that both men are sewed in weighted canvas and ready to be given the deep six."

Sam's mouth twitched. It was clever enough. There would be no evidence of the old man of the sea, nothing to connect him with Maquid. As for Lyman, he had last been placed at Haddamsport's railroad station, alive. It wasn't likely that anyone knew of his return to Sam's boat. Even if suspicions were aroused, they could be met by a bland denial, and nothing could be proved to the contrary. The ocean was wide and deep.

On the other hand, the disposal of Lyman's body took him off the spot he'd been in. Neither Broom nor Varden could manage a frame without incriminating themselves now. He shook himself mentally, fighting the thought of Lyman's body sliding into the fathomless deep. He turned back to Eli Broom.

"How did they get you so easily last night?"

The detective salvaged a butt from the ashtray. "It wasn't that easy. I followed Nora and Casper back here, after you ducked out on me, but then the dog stepped in and cornered me. I like dogs, but I don't like that one. He's a man-eater. I worked up a good sweat holding him off until Varden collared him."

Sam nodded. Beyond the window, the sunlit ocean was empty. He stretched out on the bed again and waited.

The afternoon wore on. It grew hot in the bedroom, and the sea took on a burnished look. Toward dusk, he heard the throb of the Panther's engine again as the schooner returned to her anchorage. He wondered about Ferne, and tried to guess what Nora and Casper Varden were doing. Eli Broom slept.

It was almost dark before life returned to the house. On the first floor, a radio phonograph filled the air with a Brahms concerto, and presently there were footsteps beyond the door and sounds that indicated the dog was being led away. A moment later the door was opened and Nora came in, carrying a supper tray.

The tray held more sandwiches and coffee. Sam watched her wryly as she closed the door behind her with the heel of her white suede shoe and glanced at Eli Broom.

"Mr. Varden wants to talk to you," she said. "Hello, Sam. Feeling better?"

Broom sat up and grinned. "Does his highness come up here, or am I free to go below for this chat?"

"He's waiting downstairs."

"With shotgun, poison, or blunt instrument?"

Nora frowned and put the tray down on the table near the bed. She wore a white sharkskin suit that set off her ripe figure to every advantage. A piece of costume jewelry winked on the lapel of her jacket. Her bronze hair was braided into a regal coronet, and she looked, S thought, as if she were ready for a gala evening at any of the North Shore's harbor resorts.

Shrugging, Broom left the room and shut the door behind him. Sam waited silently until Nora turned to him with a smile.

"Poor Sam," she said. "You must be starved. And you look terrible." She poured coffee for them both and waved for him to sit down on the bed beside her. "Cat got your tongue, darling?"

"Not quite. I'm just wondering. . . ."

"About me?"

"You're quite at home here, Nora."

"Sam, don't be such a fool," she said petulantly. "Surely you realize that I've got to do everything possible to lessen Varden's suspicions of me. Where would we be if I were a prisoner, too? We wouldn't stand a chance then." She pitched her voice lower, more urgently. "It's just that Varden must think I'm with *him,* darling. Otherwise, I'll never be able to help you." Again, with another change of manner, she became arch and pouted. "You don't even want to kiss me, do you? You never behaved like this before."

"I've never been in such a jam before."

She patted his hand. "Don't worry. Leave it to me, darling. We're getting out of this tonight, just you and I. Now kiss me and eat your supper. I fixed it myself."

He was surprised at his own reluctance, where once he had dreamed in torments of frustration about her. Nora's kiss held a vehemence that made it more than a perfunctory gesture. And then she suddenly drew back, her eyes oddly veiled. Smoothing her skirt, she stood up.

"You've changed, Sam. You don't love me any more."

He said nothing.

"It's that girl, isn't it? It's Ferne Dolson."

Sam said: "I'm just thinking that what we're doing isn't quite appropriate to Lyman's funeral."

She stared, her eyes wide, and then she smiled. "I keep forgetting you're a man of principles. For myself, I don't want to think about Lyman. He was thoroughly weak, and in the end it cost him his life. He should never have gotten into this if he didn't have the courage to go through with it. I made a mistake when I married him, Sam; I told you that. Now I just want to forget him."

"Who killed him?" Sam asked.

"I don't know."

"Was it Varden?"

"I'm not sure."

"Why did you and Varden come back to Maquid last night?"

Nora said: "We were looking for Lyman, of course. Don't raise your voice, darling. I talked Varden into questioning Broom downstairs, just so we could be alone for a few minutes. We don't have too much time. I can't help you about last night, simply because I don't know what happened. If I did, I would tell you. You believe me, don't you?"

"Sure," Sam said. "Every word."

Nora flushed. "I know how it must look to you. But I told you it was Lyman's idea, in the first place."

"Even," Sam said quietly, "to go cruising with Amos Butterick?"

Nora looked angry. She turned away, standing by the window to stare at the mist that enveloped the cove. The surf on the rocks below the house was little more than a complacent swish of ebbing tide. The room itself was almost dark, but her hair was alive with bronze and copper tints. When she turned back to him, her eyes looked luminous in the shadows, her face smiling and lovely.

"So you know that much," she said.

"It took me a little time to figure it. Not that I can understand it yet, even though I know what happened. I just didn't think things like that were done so blatantly. Butterick took you out of that dreary, small-town existence you once described to me, Nora, and gave you a taste for luxury. You threw him over for me, and then decided to marry Lyman. Yet you remained on friendly terms with Butterick all that time, perhaps all the time you and I were together, too."

"Amos was understanding. He was so much older than I, Sam. He considered me as a daughter. Or almost so. He fancied himself as a modern-day Pygmalion, transforming me from a sulky country girl to the Nora you fell in love with. He understood, when I married Lyman. He understood about you, too."

"Did he keep on giving you money, too?"

"Of course. All three of us were on the best of terms. You're so conventional, Sam, you don't understand these things. It was perfectly natural for Amos to invite Lyman and me for a cruise."

"And perfectly natural, I suppose, for you and Lyman and Varden to turn on him, imprison him, and torture him to death."

Nora said: "Sam, don't be so beastly about it. It was Lyman's scheme, not mine. Once started, I couldn't do anything about it. They didn't tell me anything until it was too late." She looked at him curiously. "When did you first figure it out—about Amos Butterick, I mean?"

Sam shrugged. "I didn't know who the old man was. I'd never met Butterick, you remember. Never even saw a picture of him. And he certainly never made any public appearances that I knew of. I didn't suspect his identity until I saw that photograph aboard the Panther, with a group of men on her deck. Casper Varden wasn't in the picture, though he claims to own her. But there was the old man I'd found. It began to fall together then, the first piece of the puzzle, anyway. Later, in Haddamsport, I checked the yacht registry books at the local club and learned that the Panther's owner was Butterick. It clicked, then. It made sense, and fitted with you and Lyman. It was obvious that you two, and Varden, had been Butterick's guests—that this house and the boat were really all Butterick's properties. And it was equally obvious that the old man had been lured up here by you three, either as a kind of kidnaping stunt or to extort money from him."

"Leave me out of it, Sam," Nora said. "I said I didn't know what their plans were."

"Who is Varden, anyway?"

"Lyman knew him. He was employed by Amos, too. I don't know in what capacity—some sort of business manager, I think."

"The steel business?"

"Gray market steel. Black market everything, during the war and afterward, too."

"So most of Butterick's money was made illegally?"

"I suppose so."

"You knew about it?"

"I learned about it, gradually."

"And you told Lyman," Sam stated.

"Yes, I did."

"I can figure the rest, too. Butterick made a fortune during the war and immediately afterward, and most of his deals were for cold cash. There was nothing he could do with it without getting into trouble with the federal government over income taxes. He couldn't very well get into the stock and bond markets, he couldn't use an ordinary bank account or even a deposit box to hide his cash, because all those places are accessible to investigating agents. He had to keep the cash, and he had to hide it, and that's why he bought Maquid and built this house. Right?"

Nora nodded. "He put this property in Varden's name, though. He trusted Casper thoroughly, and paid him well to keep that trust. It was Lyman who first thought of raiding Maquid to find the hiding place for the money."

"So there never was a treasure, or anything like that."

Nora's smile was tight. "Just cold cash, Sam."

"And none of you knew where it was?"

"No."

"And the old man never told anyone, of course."

Nora smiled again. "Not even me."

"So you all went to work on him to find where it was hidden."

"Not me," she said again. "Lyman and Casper."

"And what was the plan if and when you found the money?"

Nora shrugged. "A South American cruise. An announcement to the papers that Mr. Butterick and his guests, Mr. and Mrs. Cameron, and so forth, were bound for a six-months' sail in Southern waters. On the way, of course, Lyman and Varden planned to drop Butterick overboard and then announce the regrettable accident. The money would never enter the picture. That was their idea, anyway. Lyman was to sail the Panther, but his nerve broke when Butterick escaped and you showed up. He was terribly afraid of you, Sam. Now Casper plans for you to take Lyman's place and navigate and sail the Panther as her captain. He feels sure he can talk you into it for a reasonable profit. I told him, though, that it wouldn't work."

"But he can't sail until he gets the money, is that it?"

"He's sure you have it."

"And since Nate failed, you're supposed to get the information from me?"

Nora laughed softly. "Something like that. Casper is a fool, in many ways. He doesn't know you like I do, Sam."

"What happens if he doesn't find the money, after all?"

Nora said: "He'll kill you."

"And you?"

She shrugged. "I don't know."

"He won't get it," Sam said. "Not from me, anyway."

Nora's eyes glistened with a light all their own as she moved toward him in the shadows.

"But you do know where it is, don't you, Sam?"

"Yes," he said. "I know."

Chapter Fifteen

ELI BROOM DID NOT COME BACK. THE EVENING darkened into night, and a muggy calm descended over the sea. Beyond the windows, a white fog made the darkness luminous. There was no sound from the surf at the base of the bluff now, and the ebbing tide left the jagged rocks exposed far below.

Sam waited. He had showered and painfully shaved the stubble of beard on his bruised face, and now he was fully dressed in dungarees and sneakers once more. For a time, the sound of the Brahms concerto went on and on, repeated a dozen times on the automatic record player.

With Nora's departure, the dog was again placed on guard in the outer room. Sam finished the sandwiches and coffee and then forced himself to lie quietly in the dark. It was strange, he thought, how Nora had left him unmoved. Perhaps she was telling the truth when she claimed to be innocent in this affair, and perhaps she was going along on nerve alone, trying to bolster her own morale as well as his own. He wondered what went on inside her. She had never loved Lyman, that was sure. He went back in his memory to the things she had told him of her childhood and tyrannical father. The basic clay had been there for Butterick to mold from the very start, and he wondered that he himself had been so blind in the past, giving himself up to a year of self-torment. He no longer remembered what he had hoped to recapture by seeing her again.

From beyond the door came a soft whispering and then the sounds of the dog being removed again. He stood up and waited. A full minute went by before he heard the soft metallic slide of the bolt being released.

Nora came in. She had changed her white suit for

something dark, either black or blue, and she held a thin
pullover sweater for him of black wool. In her left hand
she held a leather handbag. In the darkness she kissed
him, lightly.

"Darling."

"Nora, you're taking a chance. What happened to
Broom?"

"No one is in the house now. It's nice of you to be
concerned about me."

"I don't want you to get hurt."

Her breath fanned his cheek. "I won't be, Sam. You'll
see to that. Put on this sweater, darling. You won't be
seen so easily."

"Are we going somewhere?"

"We're getting out of here."

He followed her, pulling on the thin sweater a.. ˈ
ent. The door to the corridor was ajar. A light shone
dimly on the first floor, illuminating the stairs. Nora took
his hand and drew him quickly down the steps; her fingers
were smooth and cold.

The fog was a thin white wall beyond the open doorway. The terrace looked dim and wet in the faint light. No
one was out there. He followed Nora, his sneakers silent
on the stones, and then moved up beside her when they
reached the path that wound through the woods to the
anchorage.

They had gone only a short way when Nora paused.
All around them was the fog and the tall pines, dripping
moisture. From across the headland came the distant mur-
muring of surf, but it was beyond the walls of mist that
isolated them here. Sam kept listening, for the dog, for the
crunch of Nate's boots. Nothing happened. Nora's hand
touched his face and he turned to her.

"Now what?"

"That's up to you. They took the sails off the Holiday,
you know, but I got them back; they were hidden in the
woods. I don't know what happened to the sailbag, though.
I couldn't find it. I just dumped the sails into the cockpit.
We can leave any time you say, darling. Just the two of
us."

"You've arranged things nicely."

Nora giggled softly. "They're busy at the monastery—with picks and shovels. All three of them—Casper, Nate and Eli Broom. They're looking for Amos' money."

"Did you send them up there?"

She giggled again. "I told them you dropped a hint to me this afternoon. That's why Varden let me talk to you, you know. He thought you would trust me." Nora's voice was reproachful. "I didn't want him to think I was totally useless, and anyway, I had this scheme in mind—to get them out of the way so that you and I could leave this awful place."

"With or without the money?" Sam asked.

"Darling. Whatever you say."

Sam said: "All right. Let's go."

The path twisted before them like a serpentine tunnel through the fog. He moved swiftly, aware of Nora lagging behind, but not slackening his pace. He hadn't planned to escape, but it occurred to him that if he and Nora turned up missing, Varden might decide that further search for Ferne Dolson was useless. He hoped that Ferne had gotten off the Point by now and reached Haddamsport. He could take Nora and the money there, and then decide what to do. There was the question of Lyman's murderer, but perhaps it would be best, after all, to turn everything over to the police, with the money, and take the chance that he would come out of it all right. But beyond getting to Haddamsport and making sure Ferne was safe, he made no definite plans, feeling that events would take care of themselves.

The cove was quiet, deserted. The fog moved in thin tendrils over the water, coiling low over the channel beyond. Overhead the stars were clearly visible, although it was too early for last night's moon to reappear. At her usual anchorage was the Panther, her portholes dark, her canvas neatly furled. He cut around the pier and made his way to the beach, with Nora at his heels. Ferne's lobster boat was still there, but the canvas had been pulled away from over the engine and he needed no examination to know that Nate had effectively put it out of commission.

Nora tugged at his sleeve. "I thought we were going to use the Holiday."

"We are."

He started back along the beach to where she was moored. Nora hurried after him again.

"Darling. Sam."

"Yes?"

"Are we going without the money?"

"We'll take it," he said.

"Where is it? May I see it?"

"Later," he said.

"But it's not on the boat. Lyman didn't have it with him." She spoke to Sam's back as he patiently loosened e forward spring line. "It wasn't aboard when Casper l Nate came back here later, looking for you la*t ght."

Sam straightened. "Are you sure?"

"Well, I . . ." She followed him aboard, stumbling a little among the tangled canvas of the jib and catching herself on a stay. "Sam, I don't think they even looked! But where did you hide it?"

"Help me with these sails," he said.

He didn't dare use the lantern in the cabin, remembering that the anchorage was visible from the monastery. No point in warning Varden and Nate, if Nora were telling the truth and they were up there. The darkness and fog made the task of bending on the sails rather formidable, and Nora's impatience didn't make the job easier. The Holiday's bow pulled away from the dock with the tug of the ebbing tide. There was a faint breeze, too light to dispel the mists, but it would be enough to let the sloop glide out of the anchorage. He worked fast, feeling the pressure of time, sliding the wet canvas onto the tracks by touch alone. Nora's fumbling hindered him, and he remembered that she had always been more interested in the social aspects of yacht clubs than in the boats themselves.

It was done at last. He let the sheet run loose and felt under the cockpit seats for the tiller. It wasn't there. He searched everywhere, with Nora anxiously following his moves.

"What are you looking for?" she asked. "Can't you find the money?"

"We can't sail without the tiller. Nate must have taken it ashore with the sails."

"Oh, Lord. I forgot it. It was too heavy for me to carry, anyway. It must be back in the woods where I found your sails."

She told him where to find it, behind a boulder just beyond where the trail entered the pines. "I'll wait here, darling."

He was gone about five minutes. In the darkness and the fog he had a few bad moments, trying to locate the spot, but at last he had it, and the tiller was there, buried under a little pile of pine needles.

Nora wasn't on deck when he returned to the boat. The boom made a faint slatting noise as the faint breeze tugged at the mainsail, and the Holiday made uneasy, restless movements, as if anxious to get away. No more than he, Sam thought. Then he saw the dim yellow wand of light probing under a corner of the cabin door and he dropped the tiller in the cockpit and moved forward.

"Nora, douse it!" he called urgently.

The light went out. He opened the sliding door and stepped down into the cabin and then shut the door behind him. Light flared as Nora switched on the battery lamp again. The leather curtains over the ports were drawn tight, making the lighted cabin relatively secure from probing eyes. But what captured his attention was the condition of the place.

It had been searched when he first arrived at Maquid, but not like this. Now it looked as if some frantic animal had ripped and torn at every conceivable hiding place in the boat. In the five minutes of his absence, the bunks had been stripped and the mattresses flung about and ripped open, their woolly stuffing scattered on the deck in heaps and tangles. The forward lockers were open and his blueprints—which he had vaguely hoped to work on, but never had—were tumbled in loose rolls on the port bunk.

among a heap of his extra clothing and cans of food from the galley. He didn't permit himself a glance at the opposite bunk except in the most ordinary way, in the course of his startled examination of the chaos Nora had made. The sliding panels under that bunk, concealing the baggage compartment and where he had hidden Lyman's suitcase, were still tightly shut, as if Nora hadn't suspected the space behind the panels.

Nora stood watching him, smiling oddly, a giggle deep in her throat. A cord of muscle stood out unpleasantly along one side of her neck, and her carefully braided red hair was disheveled.

"I've been looking for the money,'" she said. "Darling, it isn't here."

His voice slapped at her. "Couldn't you wait?"

"I was curious . . . all those hundreds of thousands . . ."

"We're not going to keep it," he said. "Did you think I was going to keep it with you?"

"Sam, don't be angry. I couldn't help it. Anyway, it isn't here!"

He didn't want to look at her. She was breathing fast, and she stood much too close to him. He wondered for a moment if he should shove off before checking to see if Lyman's bag was still safe, and then decided that if anything went wrong, it would defeat his purpose to leave Maquid Point without the money. Only by voluntarily turning the cash over to the police could he hope to convince them of his story, and of his own part in the affair.

Nora was suddenly quiet when he dropped to his knee and pushed aside the sliding panel under the starboard bunk. His own grips were still there: the blue canvas bag, the heavily grained pigskin Gladstone inherited from his father. He pulled them out, one after the other, not looking back at Nora, who stood close behind him. Then he reached farther back and felt the smooth leather carrying-handle of Lyman's suitcase and hauled it out.

"That's it," Nora said quickly. "I recognize it."

Her eyes were unnaturally bright, like highly polished,

"No?"

"You won't kill me, Nora."

She smiled. "You might be surprised, darling."

"I'm already surprised."

"I know you wouldn't tell the others, not even when Nate did those ugly things to you. Poor darling. But you knew they weren't going to kill you, because Varden needs you to sail the Panther. But I don't need you, Sam. I could do without you. It would be better if it were the two of us, but I could go along alone. I'd have the money to console me, sweetheart."

"Put away that gun."

"Where is the money?"

"Put it away!"

"Sam," she said.

She was going to shoot him. He knew it, as suddenly and surely as he knew the sick laughter bubbling in him, a kind of insane amusement at the things he had once thought, and the things he knew now. The laughter came out of him, and Nora stared, bewildered. And then he jumped for her gun.

He closed one hand over it and with the other he caught at her left wrist to force both her hands down and around behind her back. The gun didn't go off. But her left hand came free and her nails raked livid lines of fire across his cheek. The next moment she threw herself forward, her body alive with unsuspected strength. Her braids came undone and she shook her head savagely, panting, to toss her hair from her eyes. Sam hung on to the gun. With the bunk behind her, she had the advantage of leverage and used it to thrust him slightly backward, the while he struggled to work the revolver down; but it was caught between them, its muzzle pointing upward, and for the briefest instant it pointed directly under his jaw. He yanked hard then, and Nora gasped with sudden pain and changed her tactics, suddenly going limp and falling away from him.

He fell with her, sprawling on the narrow cabin floor. The sloop rocked with their violent movements. His fingers inched higher over the gun, closing over the barrel now, then reaching farther to pull her finger loose from the trigger guard. Nora gasped and bit at his ear, tried to boost her knee between his thighs, and then cried out with a whimper of pain as he slammed her down angrily and held her down with his weight upon her. The gun came loose and he held it for an instant before flipping it across the floor into the open compartment under the bunk.

Nora's arms clinched around his neck then. When he tried to rise, she held him down, while her laughter touched him and her lips gasped his name.

"Sam. You hurt me, darling."

"Let me up."

"Sam, I love you."

"Sure. Now that you haven't got the gun."

She giggled. He felt her writhe under him. He twisted, ng to free her arm from around his neck. When he ed his head, her lips sought his.

"Don't go away without me," she breathed. "Sam, I'll be good. I'll behave. Let's get the money and go."

"No."

"Darling, I . . ."

"No."

"Not for anything?"

"No."

"You don't love me now, do you?"

"No."

"It's Ferne Dolson, isn't it? She's changed you."

"You did it yourself," he said.

"Darling . . ."

"Behave."

He forced her arms from around his neck at last and leaned back, on his knees, then pulled himself upright beside the bunk. Nora didn't move, sprawling there before him. She was breathing heavily, and her lipstick had smeared and her red hair was tangled about her face. She smiled, making no attempt to rearrange her skirt.

"Sam, aren't you silly?" she whispered. "There's so much we could do together. Why shouldn't we take the money? It doesn't belong to anybody, it certainly never belonged to Butterick legally, and now that he's dead, no

one can claim it. Nobody even knows about it, really, and
those who do, don't count. You could handle them. You
could handle the money, Sam, I couldn't."

"Get up," he said.

He walked around her and kneeled beside the bunk to
retrieve the gun. He'd feel better with it, he decided,
because now he wasn't leaving, not until he discovered
who had the money.

Nora said persistently: "You do know where it is. You
lied to me. That suitcase was just to tease me, wasn't it?
I'm sorry I behaved so badly, darling. But you do have
the money?"

"No," he said. "Not any more."

He found the gun and stood up. Nora looked at it, then
at his face. He became aware of the stinging lines of
scratches, and he took a handkerchief and patted at
streaks of blood on his cheek. Nora smiled. She seemed
be listening for something.

"They're coming," she said.

He listened, too. He heard nothing but the tide and the
creak of the lines and the loose flap of the sails. He
reached out and picked up the electric lantern that had
somehow escaped destruction. His hand was shaking. He
listened again, and this time he heard the scrape of footsteps on the dock, and then a soft footfall as someone
stepped into the cockpit. The Holiday sank a little lower
under the added weight of the newcomer.

He looked at Nora. She shook her head, silently. He
got a better grip on the gun and waited.

The cabin door opened and Casper Varden stepped in.

Instantly, Nora screamed: *"Kill him, Sam!"*

The shock of her voice startled him, but he didn't pull
the trigger. Varden was unarmed. His hands were empty.
He was wearing a blue yachting cap with its visor pulled
down straight over his thick dark brows; a dark blue scarf
was knotted at his throat. His pale eyes jerked over the
disheveled cabin, touched briefly on Nora as she crouched
behind Sam, and then looked at Sam again.

"We are all in the soup," he said quietly.

"Sam," Nora whispered urgently. "Don't wait!"

be. I don't know if he's dead yet, but the fire will get him. I left him in the house. Nobody will know who or what he was in another ten minutes. He killed my dog."

Sam said: "You can't leave Broom there, if he's alive."

"It's done," Varden said sharply. "Get the dory, Nate. We've wasted enough time already."

Nate said: "Put up the popgun, Cameron."

He hesitated. They were too sure of themselves; their plans were made, and he stood alone against these three, knowing there was no pity in any of them; if he interfered or delayed, he would join Broom in the holocaust sweeping Maquid Point. On the other hand, he couldn't leave Broom and make himself a party to the detective's death.

"Suppose Ferne doesn't have the money?" Sam asked.

Varden smiled. "It is evident to us that you and Ferne together took a hand in our game. You, or Ferne, or both of you know where the money is now. We are certain that Lyman turned it over to you before he died, and at that point you decided to keep it and enlisted Ferne's aid to that end. But there need be no differences between us. There is enough for all, and it would be folly to allow greed to be the cause of losing everything." The man's voice hardened suddenly. "Whether you wish it or not, we are all partners now. You and Ferne, together. If you don't talk, Ferne will. Nate will make her. But there is no need to decide at once. . . . Nate, the dory, please. ⹀₂ must hurry."

Nate, cradling the shotgun under his elbow, held out his big, horny hand. "The popgun, mate. Let's have it."

Afterward, Sam wasn't sure what helped him make his decision. Every instinct revolted at leaving Broom behind. And since the success of Varden's scheme depended on eliminating anyone who could talk to the police . . .

"Here you are," he said.

He flipped the gun toward Nate, throwing it above and beyond the man's outstretched hand, toward his face. Nate ducked instinctively, and Sam spun on his heels and ran. He heard Nora's outraged cry and Nate's bellow, but he didn't look back. He was across the dock and beyond the beach, running low toward the dark shrubbery and the

path, before the shotgun roared. Nothing touched him.
There was a pattering of pellets in the brush to his right,
and then he was on the hard gravel path, with better
footing. In a moment he reached the woods, running
uphill toward the house on the opposite beach. There were
no other shots.

Smoke drifted thickly through the misty pines, curling
low over the ground. But the light of the fire showed him
the path, and now he could see that the woods were
aflame, too, the pines exploding with deafening roars,
consumed by flame from ground to crown in a vast orgy
of destruction. Waves of heat beat at him. At the top of
the rise he slowed and looked back, but no one was
behind him. The fire now lay directly across his path; he
struck off to the right, through the underbrush.

The big house was already aflame in one wing. He
hugged the edge of the bluff and raced on, the flames
closing in a solid wall behind him. The smoke was thicker,
more pungent, stinging his eyes and burning in his throat.

"Broom!" he called.

The fire roared in reply. He moved around to the front
terrace. The tall French doors stood open, and the long
curtains flapped crazily in the draft. Inside, the first
tongues of flame licked across the doors. Sparks showered
down, ashes swirled. A shadow humped and crawled
painfully across the terrace to where Sam paused. It was
Broom. The man was battered almost beyond recognition,
his clothes scorched, his hair singed, his eyes swollen shut.
Sam swung down and lifted him, hiking the man's limp
frame over his shoulder and retreating from the heat of
the fire. Beyond the terrace, the ground dropped sharply
down to the rocky beach, and he slid and stumbled and
all but fell to the water's edge. A long line of white
combers arched into the darkness and the fog.

"Put me down," Broom gasped. "It's no use."

He went on until he stood at the base of the bluff on
which the house was built. The beach was exposed at low
tide, and the steep cliff sheltered them from the heat and
burning glare of the house. Not until then did he ease the
other man to the sand.

His hands came away sticky with blood. In the flicker of light, he looked at Broom's battered gray face.

"Nate shot you?"

Broom shook his head. "Knife. He's after Ferne now. He'll kill her. They figure she's got the money."

"Has she?" Sam asked.

"I don't know. . . . Better find her. I'm all right here."

He wasn't all right. He was dying. Sam straightened. He looked back at the peak of Maquid Hill. Dimly through the curtains of red fire he saw the bleak broken walls of the monastery. He couldn't cross the point by going inland. To get to Ferne's house, he'd have to skirt the beach, and even then, the fire was encroaching rapidly to the water's edge.

There was nothing more he could do for Broom. Out at sea, a motor throbbed and a shaft of light tried to pierce the fog and smoke, only to be dissipated by the red glare. Sam turned and trotted along the beach to the eastern extremity of the headland.

The fire was a wall of insane fury, blocking his way. To his left as he faced southward, the reef that tongued farther into the sea showed in streaks of sullen white that broke over sand and rock. He might be able to wade out on it and encircle the fire that way. He had no choice. He had to do it.

The water was cold, swirling above his knees and then his hips. Overhead, through the streamers of fog and smoke, he could see the stars, cold and aloof. He waded on, searching for the far edge of the burning woods. It was strange how swiftly he felt isolated from the promontory. The tide had changed, and he could feel its cold fingers tug at his legs with new strength. He looked back once at Varden's house, and saw it as a scarlet skeleton atop the bluff, its wings outlined in flame for a vivid instant before it collapsed in a shower of bursting sparks.

The motorboat throbbed again, circling somewhere out to sea. He looked for it, pushing cautiously southward toward a dark edge of sandy beach where the fire was halted. He saw its lights, not too distant. Voices shouted, and he wondered about Dr. McReadie, whether the man had an attack of civic virtue and had called the police to come here.

The ledge was slippery with barnacles. In a few minutes, a light glimmered where he could look down the southern shore of the Point. It was Ferne's house. The tug of the tide all but halted his wading progress. He decided to swim, impatient and anxious over Ferne, and shoved free to the reef, stroking powerfully for the beach and the solitary light of her house.

And then the light went out. The dark sea closed around him. The bubbling tide swept him into the outer night.

Chapter Seventeen

THE COLD WATER BURBLED AND RAN WITH A life all its own, fighting him back. For a moment he paused, rolling to look up at the stars that gleamed faintly through the smoky mist. A lurid red light filled the sky over the burning headland.

The light in Ferne's house didn't come on again. He swam on, striving for the sand dunes that resisted the fire. The motorboat was gone, presumably circling northward again. But the note of its engine was replaced by a deeper sound. Dark and sleek and ghostly, the Panther glided by, her black hull only slightly blacker than the dark water. Then she was gone, the sound of the auxiliary muffled by the tide and the cottony, smoky fog.

He seemed to have been swimming forever, circling the patch of burning shore, before the dark beach loomed ahead. Somewhere to the right he heard the crash of breakers, but ahead there seemed to be a safe landing, even if it was among the rocks. He guessed he was a quarter of a mile east of Ferne's house, and now he could see the shimmer of reflected flames in the windows, mirroring the fire on the hill. The Panther was out of sight, but it would be tied up on the other side of the house, he was sure. He rested a moment, letting the tide sweep him closer inshore.

Presently his knee scraped a barnacled ledge and he stood up, sucking air. He felt exhausted. He was on a small point of jumbled rock. Shadows moved and swayed in the rough confusion ahead. To his right, a mass of sea-worn granite lifted dark overhead, and he felt his way shoreward along its base. The sea gurgled and whispered all around him, forming dark secret pools here and there, and a miniature surf that broke with little crashing ripples.

Far to the north, beyond the headland, he thought he saw the bright shaft of a spotlight, but it was gone in a moment. There was no other sign of the boats Varden had seen. He gave grudging credit to Varden for creating the confusion of fire to cover his escape.

If Ferne really was still at home, the Panther would be tied up at her lobster dock there. Ferne might have seen them coming, however, and vanished into the dunes; or they might have surprised her with consequences he didn't care to imagine . . .

He was only a few yards from shore, still waist-deep in the dark water, when Nate hailed him.

There were no words—just the sound of chuckling triumph. He halted in the deep shadow, searching the darkness. Only the jumble of rocks and salt water pools surrounded him. He saw no one.

Then Nate's voice jeered again.

"Up here, chum. I figured you would make for this spot. We got things to settle, you and me."

The voice came from above, but he realized it too late. There came a sound from the granite ledge, and then a dark shape hurtled down to land on his back with crushing force.

Driven to his knees, he fell headlong into dark water. Something slashed his arm and left a ribbon of pain. Nate had a knife. He stumbled aside, twisted to face him. For an instant neither moved, and the roiled water subsided.

Nate bulked dark and malevolent against the red glare. He could see the man's grin and the long, wet finger of light on the knife.

"You can't get away," Nate whispered. "You ain't goin' on the Panther. Just one of us is going to run that schooner, and it won't be you, no matter what Varden thinks."

Sam thought of his other encounters with Nate; he thought of Eli Broom and old Butterick. The anger returned to him, and he knew he was not going to retreat this time. Nate couldn't seem to stop talking. He was content not to rush things, savoring this moment and rolling the gloating words on his tongue.

"We got Ferne. We'll get the money, too. Don't worry about her, matey. I'll take care of her—soon as I finish you."

The big man tensed, ready with the knife. Sam braced himself, but the ledge was slippery underfoot, and the icy water around his waist hampered him. It helped to slow Nate, as well. The knife slashed wildly at his chest, and he knocked down the man's arm, driving the blow aside. Nate stumbled and Sam threw all his weight into a hard right. His knuckles crunched and Nate cried out and splashed into the troubled water. His fist caught the side of Sam's head with a wild blow and they went under together.

Half floating on hands and knees, Sam felt the tide roll him over while the sharp edge of a submerged rock cut his back. He straightened, rising to the surface to see Nate before him, confused, his back turned. He jumped, the water a white froth around him, and landed on Nate's shoulders. The big man went down, hands and arms outspread. The knife went glimmering and wriggling into the dark of the pool, lost for good. Sam whipped his left arm around the other's head and yanked hard. Nate made a strangling sound and tried to heave erect. Sam felt himself lifted on the other's back and flung forward; but he didn't lose his armlock, and they crashed down into the water together again. He tightened the squeeze on the other's throat. Nate's legs thrashed, scissoring backward around his own. Sam held his breath and dragged the big

man under, hauling his grip tighter. The flowing tide
picked them up and bumped them into deeper water at
the base of the granite outcropping.

Rolling over and over in a fantastic sort of slow motion, they sank deeper into the bottom of the rock-bound
pool. For a few moments longer Nate thrashed about,
seeking escape, while Sam's lungs screamed for air. Even
when Nate went limp and a stream of bubbles washed up
to the surface, he was reluctant to let go. Eventually it was
that or drown with the man, and he released him, scram-
bling up to the surface. Nate's body floated slowly after.

The dark air felt colder than the water, rushing into
him. He gulped it, chest heaving, and floundered slowly to
the shallow edge of the pool. Nate's body broke the surface, then sank again as the tide pulled at it. He did not
reappear. . . .

Shadows moved on the rocks above. He staggered to his
feet, aware of a desperate need to find Ferne. A voice
hailed him.

"Cameron!"

Light stabbed narrowly from a pocket torch. He was
too tired to duck out of the way. The light jumped from
rock to rock, from pool to pool. It blazed into his eyes.
Slowly he hauled himself out of the water toward it.

Varden's voice was calm and pleased.

"So you killed him," the man said.

He stood, squat and ugly, behind the light, a gun in his
right hand. Beside him was Nora, her red hair braided
again, a peculiar smile matching the pleasure in Varden's
words. Ferne Dolson stood a little to one side.

"Darling," Nora said. "Darling, that was magnificent."

He looked at Ferne. *They've got her,* he thought. Her
dark hair fell tumbled about her shoulders; her lips were
pale. She didn't smile as Sam climbed toward her. She
wore a dark skirt, no stockings, and a loose-fitting, cardi-
gan sweater. She looked young and helpless, no longer
sullen. Her eyes appealed to him.

Varden was pleased. "You have saved me an unpleasant
chore, Cameron. Nate knew too much to be left behind,
and demanded too much of my generosity. I am not a

generous man. But as it is, the four of us should get along nicely on the Panther."

"Sure," Sam said. "Just fine."

"Everything is satisfactory," Varden nodded. "Ferne had the money, and now I have it. All that remains is to be off with it."

"With the cops at our heels?"

"You can get us to sea without running into them. You will cooperate, since Ferne is with us. I have no faith to spare in human nature; I trust no one; but we either sink or swim from this moment onward." His voice grew brisk. "Now is the time to run for it. The police are on the opposite side of the point. The fire has destroyed anything they might have found there. But while they are occupied, we will make off. I suggest we hurry, Cameron. You may go ahead with Ferne. Nora and I will be directly behind you."

Chapter Eighteen

FERNE'S HAND WAS LIGHT AND COOL IN HIS AS they crossed the grassy dunes toward the house. Heavy white rollers crashed along the southerly shore, beyond the outline of Ferne's house on its high pilings. The Panther was still out of sight behind it, and now and then a thick streamer of smoke from the hilltop wiped out everything, filling their lungs with its acrid pungency. Presently he said:

"You should have gone to Haddamsport. You'd have been safe."

"Perhaps I didn't want to be safe," she said quietly.

"How did you find the money?"

"I searched the Holiday after I left you. I was— curious."

Sam said: "And you found Lyman."

"You should have warned me. Were you waiting to see if I knew he was dead? I didn't know, of course."

"Don't be angry, Ferne."

"I'm not. I'm only sorry we—I'm just sorry, that's all."

"Don't be," he said. He paused. "You're the one who took the money from the suitcase, then?"

Ferne nodded. Her fingers were tense in his hand, curled around his own, and she walked very close to him. Close behind their heels came Varden and Nora.

"I used your sailbag and then put the money in the Panther's skiff," she said. "Varden has it now. He made me tell. He said he would let Nate—that Nate would—"

Sam said: "I know. Nate is dead now." He paused. "You should have taken the money to the police in Haddamsport."

"I couldn't," she said. "I didn't know about you. You didn't mention Lyman's murder or the money. I didn't know what to think. I wondered if you were mixed up with them, after all; but I didn't want to believe it. So I went home to wait and see."

"And now you know I'm not?"

"Now I know," she said. "And now it's too late."

From behind came Nora's voice, amused. "Darling, you shouldn't be so secretive with your loves. It doesn't pay, you see. I thought a few nasty things about you, myself."

Varden said: "This discussion is futile. Hurry, please."

Ferne's house was dark when they reached the rickety wooden landing nearby. Sam hesitated, and Varden pushed the gun into his back; he went on with Ferne, winding across the plank walk that crossed the inlet. He wondered if he should try for Varden now. Once captain of the Panther and out to sea, nothing would convince the authorities that he hadn't been involved from the start. Broom was probably dead by now. Suspicion would touch Ferne, too, since everyone in Haddamsport knew of her long feud with Nate. Only by turning the money over to the police could he convince them of his story; and he didn't have the money yet. He had to go on.

The Panther was moored at the long wooden pier that had served Ferne's lobster boat. At low tide now, her hull was well below the level of the stringpiece, and only her tail spars could be visible to boats at sea; even that was doubtful, considering the smoke and fog. Every element favored Varden's plan for a quick getaway.

"We'll leave under power," Varden said. "Once clear of the shore, we'll make sail, to preserve silence. I expect your full cooperation, Cameron. I shall brook no interference at this point. I shall kill you if I must, and use Ferne to operate the boat."

Sam said: "I'm not arguing."

THE PANTHER HANDLED SMOOTHLY, HER screw making scarcely a wake under her fantail. No lights were used. Immediately on going aboard, Nora moved to the sailbag that lay on deck at the foot of the mainmast. It was the Holiday's sailbag, and the money was in it. From his station at the wheel, Sam glanced at Varden, near the port quarter, and then at Ferne. She shook her head slightly in a negative gesture. He knew she meant it was useless to make an attempt now. Varden kept a safe distance between them to guard against any surprise. And now even the fog closed down as they slipped along the shore, and there was no sign of the police boats.

Varden spoke quietly: "Get the sails up now. . . . Nora?"

Nora started, interrupted as she bent over the sailbag on the deck. Varden's voice cut sharply through the gloom.

"If you can tear yourself away from that money long enough to help, please, it would be appreciated."

"I'm not a sailor," Nora said sullenly.

"You will learn. Begin now. After all, we shall be at sea for weeks. Ferne will show you what to do."

Nora laughed abruptly. "All right, Captain Bligh. But look out when you go to sleep."

Varden was undisturbed as he turned back to Sam. "The motor, please."

The throb of the auxiliary was replaced by the soft wash of water around the schooner's bow and the quiet bubbling of her wake. The tide turned her slightly inshore. The mist was alive with flames, filled with the distant roar of the fire. The red glow touched the water with bloody fingers. The schooner surged ahead, carried forward by her way.

"The jib first," Sam said.

Ferne nodded and made a little rotary motion of her hand. Sam turned the wheel a little more to starboard and the Panther nosed on a more westerly course, heading toward the mainland along the southern shore of Maquid Point. Ferne went forward to work at the canvas. The two girls labored in mutual hostility. The wind, at best only a light breeze, was variable owing to the immense drafts created by the forest fire on Maquid. The jib flapped, filled and emptied, then suddenly caught and brought the Panther's head around with a sudden surge of momentum. Varden moved away from the rail and approached Sam.

"You are going the wrong way."

"We haven't much choice, under sail. We have to tack."

"Bring her about! We can't risk skirting the beach."

Shrugging, Sam put over the wheel. The jib luffed in another quick shift of the wind, the canvas flapping and streaming in crazy fashion. The schooner's forward progress stopped; she began to drift backward, pressed sternward against the tide.

Sam said: "The fires you set knocked hell out of the wind. It's not easy, without the motor."

"Just a moment," Varden said. "Let her drift, please."

His voice had sharpened. Sam looked at the seaward reach of Maquid Point. Lights moved with disquieting speed through the ruddy mist, and the high, keening wail of a siren sounded over the bubbling of the tide. There seemed to be two boats there now, and their running lights showed red and green in dim points of radiance. There was still a mile between them and the schooner, and it wasn't likely they had seen the Panther yet. A searchlight stabbed across the water, only to be dissipated in a smoky fog.

Varden made a quick, nervous gesture with his gun and looked forward, to Ferne and Nora. "Get the mainsail up!"

"We can't outrun them," Sam said. "Not enough breeze."

"Then start the motor again. We'll hug the shore going south toward Haddamsport, then strike for the open sea."

"How much water does the Panther draw?"

"I don't know. We must chance it. Quickly!"

Sam started the motor. The mainsail creaked up unsteadily as Ferne and Nora hauled on the lines, their strength taxed by the weight of the canvas. The sail filled at the moment the motor caught and throbbed. The Panther surged ahead again, gliding through the fog at increasing speed. Varden crossed the deck and stood beside Sam, the gun in his back.

"You are an accomplished sailor, Mr. Cameron. I will not tolerate any mistakes."

"We're damned close to the beach. I can't guarantee—"

"You must!"

The lights of the first patrol boat vanished, apparently going landward to Ferne's dock. The second one, however, came steadily westward in their wake. The searchlight still stabbed out, still useless in the cloak of fog.

"They're looking for us," Sam said.

Varden signalled to Ferne. She came aft out of the darkness to join them, her face dimly outlined in the glow of the binnacle. Her eyes gave nothing away.

"How much water is ahead?" Varden rapped.

"Not much. There's shoal where the beach curves south. Then deep water all the way down to Haddamsport. If the wind and tide are right, we might get over." Her voice was flat, dispirited. "You haven't much choice but to try, have you?"

Varden returned impatiently to the rail. He was keyed up now, his nerves on a hair trigger. Watching him, Sam knew the man was capable of anything in his desperation. Time ran out swiftly while the schooner edged along off the beach, heeling more and more with the pressure of the breeze in her towering sails. Sam studied the vast arcs of canvas that reached up through the murk and fog. The trucks seemed to be touching the remote stars above the surface mist. As he watched, the searchlight stabbed astern again, brighter now, and reflected on the white canvas; passed beyond, then swung back to turn the sail all a-glitter with radiance. They were spotted. His heart jumped with sudden excitement. But the powerboat was half a mile astern, siren wailing futilely, and the shoal was dead ahead, the white disturbance of the water visible now, beyond the bow.

He took a firmer grip on the wheel, looking at Ferne. She stood with one hand braced on a stay, staring ahead, her body plainly tensed for the schooner's death blow. Something loomed out of the water in a dark, ominous mass, a stone's throw to starboard, and slid astern.

Then they were on the bar. Water chopped restlessly all around them, and more jutting rocks shaped the surface of the sea. The schooner faltered and fell off several points to port, deflected by the sharp thrust of a tidal current. A jagged ledge slid by the quarter. Nora made a whimpering sound, quickly stifled—and then there came a grating, bumping sound as the massive keel, gliding far below the surface, touched unyielding granite. The schooner shuddered in every timber, made a sound of pain that was all her own. The masts swayed in a crazy arc through the high fog above; the sails spilled wind and flapped thunderously. Varden lunged to the engine controls and advanced the throttle full out, his face convulsed. The keel bumped again. From up forward came a sharp cracking sound as a stay parted; the vessel heeled over still farther, the decks crazily tilted—and then the shuddering ended, the Panther settled a little, and they were over, into deep water.

The dark, empty expanse of the open sea lay ahead.

Chapter Nineteen

VARDEN SAID: "I RARELY CARE FOR CALCU-
lated risks with the unknown. We are safe now. If the

other boats follow now, we have the whole wide ocean in which to lose them."

The tension was gone. Laughing softly, Nora moved forward to the sailbag at the foot of the mainmast. Ferne still stood with a firm grip on the backstay, looking ahead into the darkness, her presence almost unnoticed by Varden. Sam heard the man chuckle.

"Nate would have failed. I made a wise choice in selecting you as captain, Mr. Cameron. You did quite well."

The man was relaxed now, leaning on the rail, the gun loose in his stubby fingers. Behind them, the fiery headland dropped swiftly away. There was no further sign of the powerboat. Its searchlight was gone.

It was then that Ferne made the slight circular motion of her fingers, to starboard again. Sam eased the spokes of the wheel to the right, a sudden excitement clamoring in his mind. The very attitude of her braced figure told him she expected more. He spread his feet on deck, tensing himself—

The Panther struck without warning. Her bow hit hard, heaving up violently on the ledge Ferne knew was there. The vessel screamed in agony, the screech of her torn timbers mingling with Varden's harsh shout as the deck lurched, throwing him off his feet toward Sam. The mainmast came down with a great splintering of wood, her stays parting with sharp, vicious reports. Canvas and rigging tumbled crazily over the port side. The schooner surged ahead another few feet and halted, canted impossibly, her bows firmly gripped in the mass of rock looming ahead. Water hissed and gurgled in her bottom.

Something struck Sam's foot. It was Varden's gun. He kicked it forward toward Ferne, but he didn't stop to see if she retrieved it. Varden smashed into him and Sam's grip on the wheel was torn loose. Together they went down, sliding across the deck to the quarter rail. Varden didn't let go; the man was crazed with fear. Dimly above the pounding of the schooner, Sam heard someone scream. He smashed his fist at Varden's convulsed face as they slammed against a stanchion. The man cursed shrilly and fought back, kicking and clawing like an outraged woman. Sam hooked a leg around the stanchion as a brace against the canted deck. Water boiled only a foot away, and he was aware of a new movement of the schooner as it pounded against the black rocks that held her fast. She was filling, shifting on the ledge, grating against the granite teeth that kept her there.

Suddenly he was free. Afterward he remembered that Varden had tried to rise against the tilted deck and lost his balance. In an instant he was over the side, his figure black against the white froth behind him. The next moment there was nothing left but a scream as he pitched into the water. The schooner rolled in its cradle of rock, came to an even keel, then fell off again, smashing in death agony against the jutting ledge. Varden was caught between hull and rock. Sam just glimpsed the man's wild face and heard his despairing scream as the schooner crushed him. Then he was gone.

As if the stricken vessel knew what it had done, it now lay quietly in the grip of the ledge. The grinding ended, replaced by a steady crash and boom of nearby surf. Slowly, Sam pulled himself back to the wheel. Forward, there was nothing but jumbled wreckage, the shattered masts hidden in the tangle of canvas that spilled over into the restless dark water. He looked for Ferne and saw her lying against the rail nearby, a jagged scratch across her face. He made his way painfully toward her. Fog moved in thin streamers over the disheveled deck, while high above the stars shone down on the black sea with cold impersonality.

She was still breathing. She had been knocked out by a flying fragment of wreckage, and only the rail kept her from sliding off into the wash of the tide. Sam felt a flood of deep relief.

"Darling?"

It was Nora. She came toward him, picking her way with care across the deck. He put Ferne down and stood up.

"Sam?"

She was smiling. He wondered what she had to smile about, and then he saw that somehow she had found Varden's gun on the deck, and she held it as if she were going to use it.

"Nora, for God's sake—"

"Don't get upset, Sam. Everything is all right now."

"What are you talking about?"

"The beach is near. We can make it, you and I. Things haven't worked out the way Casper planned it, but I was never too enthusiastic about South America. I want to spend this money in the good old U.S.A. You can help me spend it, Sam."

"This is no time to think about it. Put the gun away."

"Darling, this *is* the time to think about it. There won't be any other time. You won't have another chance, you see."

"You can't make the beach through this surf."

"Yes, we can. You can do it. Just you and me, darling."

Smiling. Smiling when she looked at him, and again when she glanced at Ferne. He knew what she meant. Ferne couldn't come with them. And she wouldn't let Ferne be found on the schooner by the police, either. He felt sick. It was insane that she could still think about the money, here on this wreck, alone in the twisting fog and the hungry, whispering sea. The desolation of the boat, the death of Varden, meant nothing to her. Only the money. She was insane. Madness giggled behind her smile, behind the gun in her hand.

"Well, darling?"

He drew a deep breath. "I couldn't trust you, Nora. I'd have to sleep behind locked doors. You'd kill me, too."

She caught at the word. "Too?"

"You tried to convince me you were an innocent bystander when all this started. You blamed Lyman, you blamed Varden, and said it was their scheme, not yours, to get that money from Butterick. But it wasn't. It was your idea from the start. Everything that happened came about because you wanted it that way and talked Lyman into it, inducing him and Varden to lure old Butterick up here in the first place. It fits, Nora. It fits you."

"Darling, you shouldn't say such things."

"*You* killed Lyman. You got him into something too big for him to handle. You couldn't check his panic after Nate tortured the old man. Then I came along," Sam said bitterly. "Just at the right time. And you saw a substitute for Lyman in me. So you got rid of him."

"Sam, dear, this is nonsense."

He shook his head, a stubborn, suicidal anger in him. "In his panic, Lyman tried to do alone what he couldn't do with you. If he hadn't stumbled on Butterick and learned where the money was hidden, if he hadn't gotten his hands on it while all of you were in Haddamsport, he might never have tried it. But he did. He had the money with him at the railroad station, and he had it after Varden broke his arm with that cane. He had it when he visited Dr. McReadie and he left it there for me. He did *not* have the money when he returned to the Holiday to find me."

Sam paused. "There was some confusion among all of you about that murder. Everyone thought the others had killed Lyman. But no one knew where Lyman had ditched the money. No one but you, Nora. You gave yourself away when you pretended to help me escape and took me to the Holiday. You were surprised to learn I expected to find the money aboard. You said, 'But Lyman didn't have it with him when he came back here.' "

Sam's voice was sharp. "How could you know Lyman hadn't returned the money to the Holiday, unless you yourself had been with him in Haddamsport before I arrived? And having been with him on the Holiday, you killed him, and left him there for me to find!"

"Sam—"

"You're sick, Nora. All your life you've been guided by greed. Butterick didn't give you an unlimited purse— maybe he knew you too well, or not well enough. First you considered me a possible avenue to the wealth you wanted, and then you chose Lyman. You knew about Butterick's secret fortune in cash from black market operations after the war. You knew Varden, too. All you had to do was plant the idea in Lyman's head—poor, weak, arrogant Lyman, always skirting the fringes of the law, but too uncertain of himself to move without your urging. But when he became a danger to you, you killed him and left him on my boat to tangle me in this thing so I'd have to go along with you. But I won't."

Nora had stopped smiling. The boat lurched, and she staggered a little, but quickly recovered. Through the fog came the muted wail of a siren. Sam listened to the sound of the sea.

"It's true," Nora said. "Everything you said is true, Sam. It shouldn't make any difference. All my life I've waited for a chance like this. I thought you loved me, Sam; I thought you'd be willing to do this for me, and be happy afterward, with never a worry again. But if it makes such a difference to you, then you know what I've go to do. If I hang for one murder, I might as well hang for three."

"It's no good, Nora. We're stuck here. You can't get away. The police boats will figure where we are. They'll find us."

"We've still got time. Come with me."

"No, Nora."

"All that money, Sam!"

"No."

Her voice stiffened. "You're forcing me to do this, darling. I don't want to. But if I have to be caught here, if the police find us, they must find only one of us. Not you and Ferne. Just me."

He looked at her.

She said: "I could tell them anything, then. They'd have to believe me. I'd tell them you were all in it together, that you came here and killed Lyman yourself."

"Nora. . . ."

"I'd have to, Sam! I don't want to hang for these things."

"But you wouldn't have the money, Nora."

"Not all of it, no. But some of it. The government gives

substantial rewards for income-tax recoveries. I'd have to be content with that."

Again the schooner lurched, lifting and settling with a shuddering bump. The tide, still rising, was working her loose, lifting her and then dragging her a bit farther into deep water. It was only a matter of time until they sank, Sam thought. He heard Ferne moan and stir and saw her struggle to sit up. He wondered if he could get Nora's gun away from her; but Nora would never take Ferne along, even if he pretended to agree with her plan. Time had run out for all of them, anyway. It wouldn't work. A light blinked off the port quarter, went out, then doubled into a boat's running lamps. Nora said: "Make up your mind, Sam. Hurry."

"It's no good," he said. He watched her pale face in the mist. "Everything you did was for the money, and you've lost it." He looked beyond her. "It's gone into the sea, Nora."

She didn't believe him. Her face worked queerly in the dimness, and for a moment he thought she was going to use the gun out of sheer, vengeful spite. Then she backed across the slanting deck, cautiously, until she was a safe distance from him. Not until she was sure he couldn't jump for her gun did she venture to look around at the shattered mainmast for the sailbag.

It wasn't there.

Sam said: "It slid overboard while you were talking, Nora."

He started toward her, not looking at Ferne, who had pulled herself erect and clung to the rail. There was silence from Nora. Then a giggle.

"Darling, it couldn't have. It just couldn't!"

Abruptly she turned away and scrambled toward the tangle of canvas and shattered spars. Sam paused. Ferne moved to his side, her face white, watching Nora. The schooner groaned and shifted again, balancing precariously on the edge of the deep.

Afterwards, Sam reasoned it was Nora's frantic shifting of sails and spars that gave the Panther her final push to the bottom. He remembered seeing her drag some sail over the side with frantic, desperate strength, not believing the money was gone, forgetting everything but her desire to find it. He cried out when the schooner began to slide back off the ledge, but it was already too late. The vessel groaned once more, and sighed. The sea rose up and closed over the deck, sweeping about his legs, his thighs, and then dragging him under in a loud tumult of screaming timbers and hissing air. . . .

The cold water had greedy fingers. He didn't struggle or go down very far. When he knew he had to resist or stay under for good, he kicked powerfully and shot up again, his head breaking water over a comber. Sand scraped his knee. He felt himself picked up and hurled inshore, swung toward the beach, flung at the land as if the sea rejected him. For several moments the combers battered him until he got a footing. He turned then, searching the night, aware of the wind in the dune grass behind him.

The sea was empty. The schooner was gone. There was nothing but the coiling mists and the black, bubbling water beyond the surf.

"Ferne!" he shouted.

He saw her then, wading toward him. Somewhere offshore an engine throbbed and the searchlight stabbed across the beach. It was the police boat. There was no trace of Nora. Sam turned away and walked wearily across the beach toward Ferne.

Chapter Twenty

SUNLIGHT FILTERED THROUGH THE DUSTY courthouse window of the sheriff's office in Haddamsport. It seemed to Sam that he'd been watching the shaft of light forever as it crept from the yellow wall behind the sheriff's desk to touch the stuffed owl on a pedestal in the opposite corner of the room, and then the chair in which Eli Broom sat.

The little man had an arm in a sling, and his face was liberally bandaged. His grin was as broad as ever as he gathered up his papers from the sheriff's desk.

"Well, there you have it, gentlemen. My credentials as an agent of the Treasury Department—" he turned his grin on Sam "—and arson and triple murder, all for a lot of money we may never recover. The money was my primary interest, of course. Mr. Cameron accused me of failing to be impressed by his brother's murder, and I must apologize for that. If I came to you with the case then, Sheriff, we might never have cracked the thing. As it is, the business is closed, though I didn't do a satisfactory job."

The sheriff, a big, rawboned man who still looked uncertain and confused despite Sam's statements and Eli Broom's explanations, rubbed his jaw and sighed.

"I got some fishin' boats draggin' round the spot for the girl's body. Don't think we're going to find her. The schooner is a mess, and she's in deep water. I figure this Nora Cameron got trapped in the weight of canvas and was pulled down when the boat sank. It might take divers to recover her body. Might do it at that, if the money is down there with her."

Sam listened with only half an ear. There was a dragging emptiness in him that refused to fill up. It didn't matter what they said now, anyway. It was all over. Finding Broom alive on the patrol boat had been a welcome surprise. Broom as a Treasury agent was another surprise, but it made little difference now. Sam was in the clear. He watched the sunlight creep across the office floor.

Broom was saying: "We'll need Mr. Cameron's testimony in court, of course. What with the fire on the island and the loss of the schooner, there isn't much other tangible evidence except his statements and Miss Dolson's."

"I'll stick around as long as you need me," Sam said.

Broom smiled again. "I won't try to thank you for saving my life, Sam. But I owe you apologies for the bad moments I had to give you. Meanwhile, see Doc McReadie and get yourself fixed up a bit. If it wasn't for the doctor, things might not have worked out as they did. He's the one who got suspicious of you and finally got the police to investigate Maquid Point."

Sam nodded. He had said nothing about his last visit to McReadie. He saw no reason to blast the doctor's reputation. His one lapse could be forgotten. He wished he could forget a number of other things as easily.

Broom went on: "Anyway, you'll want to see Ferne Dolson, Sam. She's staying with the doctor for the time being. . . ."

A COOL BREEZE WASHED THE COURTHOUSE square. The same two old men sat on the same stone bench, playing, for all Sam knew, the same game of chess. Mothers strolled with baby carriages in the shade of the towering elms. A visiting artist had set up his easel and was painting the row of old sea captains' houses that flanked the west side of the square. Sam crossed the little park with a long, unhurried stride. The emptiness ached inside him. From this vantage point he could look beyond the rooftops along the harbor to the wide stretch of sparkling blue sea. A number of sails arched in dazzling white against the far horizon, and lying low against the sky was a thin smudge of smoke from the fires still smoldering on Maquid Point.

The doctor's house looked pleasantly cool on the corner of Lemon Street. Sam walked up the shaded path, aware of a decision forming inside him and a knowledge of the future that replaced the emptiness with a growing excitation. He wondered how Ferne would be—sullen, as at first, or the way she had been on the hilltop, in the monastery ruins, last night. And he wondered whether her feelings toward him had lived through the long, harrowing night.

He followed the maid down to Dr. McReadie's sitting room and found the doctor sitting there as before, his long face creased by an apologetic smile.

"Mr. Cameron, you should retain me on an annual basis as the Chinese do, paying me to keep you well. You've taken another beating, I see."

"I'll be all right now," Sam said.

"You'd just come from the courthouse?"

He nodded. It was good to sit here. Somehow his attitude had changed since yesterday, when McReadie had faced him in this same room with his gun and his greed. McReadie had no gun now, but he was even more nervous than on the other occasion. His hands trembled, closing on the arms of his chair as he leaned forward.

"Have you told them, Mr. Cameron?"

"About you?"

"About my—— about our difference of opinion last night."

"No," Sam said. "I didn't mention it."

Dr. McReadie sank back with a sigh. "Perhaps I shouldn't have been such a coward about it. I really should go to them and tell them I tried to keep the money for myself."

"What good would that do?" Sam asked.

"It would ease my conscience. I've behaved badly. I could have prevented several deaths if I'd gone to the police last night, instead of waiting as long as I did."

"I doubt if that would have changed anything," Sam said, "except to ruin yourself. You're a respected man in Haddamsport, Doctor. Everyone is entitled to one mistake. I made mine, you made yours. Now we can forget it."

McReadie sighed again. "I am deeply grateful, young man. It took me several hours to come to my senses, after you left last night. Even then, I didn't know what to do. I was afraid Ferne was mixed up in it, too, and I'd do anything to save her from harm. She's been like a daughter to me, and my son and Ferne once——"

"I know," Sam said.

"I'm glad I was not entirely too late in sending the police to Maquid. If there is anything more I can do——"

"I'd like to see Ferne, if she's here."

"She's out, just now." McReadie seemed suddenly more

at ease. A glimmer of amusement flickered in his sunken eyes. "What do you plan to do with yourself now, Sam? Ferne told me all about you last night, while you were with the police. I understand you are a boat-builder."

"I was," Sam said.

"Haddamsport needs a good boatyard. And since you will be staying until the courts clear things up, perhaps you'd consider locating your business here."

"I'll think about it," Sam said. "Where did Ferne go?"

"Of course." Dr. McReadie grinned. "She left a message for you. She said you could still buy her dinner. She said something about it being better late than never."

"Thank you," Sam said.

In a moment he was outside again, walking toward Main Street and the waterfront. He walked fast, the excitement in him controlled, though he wanted to run. McReadie had a good idea, he thought, about a boatyard in Haddamsport. He liked the town. He didn't want to go back to Long Island; he wanted to start over again here. His only assets at present were the Holiday and the designs aboard her. He could raise money somehow to get started once more. For the first time in a year, his thoughts turned to problems of new design, of the careful balance between the forces of wind and sea, of the exact shape a hull would need. . . .

And then he pushed those thoughts aside and entered Adam's Chop House. The walls were clean and shining. It was early for the dinner hour, and the place was almost empty. He saw Ferne at once, sitting at the same table as the other night. She saw him come in, and turned her face toward him and smiled. He hurried toward her, recognizing what was in her eyes. And then he sat down and reached for her hand across the table.

69–11–3